W.G. Sebald

THE EMIGRANTS

Translated from the German by Michael Hulse

Published by Vintage 2002

4 6 8 10 9 7 5 3

First published with the title *Die Ausgewanderten* by
Vito von Eichborn Verlag, Frankfurt am Main, 1993

First published in Great Britain in 1996 by
The Harvill Press

Vintage
Random House, 20 Vauxhall Bridge Road,
London SW1V 2SA

Random House Australia (Pty) Limited
20 Alfred Street, Milsons Point, Sydney,
New South Wales 2061, Australia

Random House New Zealand Limited
18 Poland Road, Glenfield
Auckalnd 10, New Zealand

Random House (Pty) Limited
Endulini, 5A Jubilee Road, Parktown 2193,
South Africa

The Random House Group Limited Reg. No. 954009

www.randomhouse.co.uk

A CIP catalogue record for this book
is availabl from the British Library

ISBN 0 099 44888 2

Papers used by Random House are natural, recyclable products made from wood grown in sustainable forests. The manufacturing processes conform to the environmental regulations of the country of origin

Printed and bound in Great Britain by
Bookmarque Ltd, Croydon, Surrey

CONTENTS

DR HENRY SELWYN 1

PAUL BEREYTER 25

AMBROS ADELWARTH 65

MAX FERBER 147

THE EMIGRANTS

W.G. Sebald was born in Wertach im Allgäu, in the Bavarian Alps, in 1944. He studied German language and literature in Freiburg, Switzerland and Manchester. In 1966 he took up a position as an assistant lecturer at the University of Manchester, settling permanently in England in 1970. He was professor of Modern German Literature at the University of East Anglia until his death in 2001.

Michael Hulse has translated Goethe's *The Sorrows of Young Werther* and Jacob Wasserman's *Caspar Hauser*, as well as the contemporary German authors Luise Rinser, Botho Strauss and Elfriede Jelinek. He is also an award-winning poet and, with John Kinsella, the editor of the literary magazine *Stand*. He lives in Amsterdam.

ALSO BY W.G. SEBALD

The Rings Of Saturn
Vertigo

DR HENRY SELWYN

And the last remnants
memory destroys

At the end of September 1970, shortly before I took up my position in Norwich, I drove out to Hingham with Clara in search of somewhere to live. For some 25 kilometres the road runs amidst fields and hedgerows, beneath spreading oak trees, past a few scattered hamlets, till at length Hingham appears, its asymmetrical gables, church tower and treetops barely rising above the flatland. The market place, broad and lined with silent façades, was deserted, but still it did not take us long to find the house the agents had described. One of the largest in the village, it stood a short distance from the church with its grassy graveyard, Scots pines and yews, up a quiet side street. The house was hidden behind a two-metre wall and a thick shrubbery of hollies and Portuguese laurel. We walked down the gentle slope of the broad driveway and across the evenly gravelled forecourt. To the right, beyond the stables and outbuildings, a stand of beeches rose high into the clear autumn sky, its rookery deserted in the early afternoon, the nests dark patches in a canopy of foliage that was only occasionally disturbed. The front of the large, neoclassical house was overgrown with Virginia creeper. The door was painted black and on it was a brass knocker in the shape of a fish. We knocked several times, but there was no sign of life inside the house. We stepped back a little. The sash windows, each divided into twelves panes, glinted blindly, seeming to be made of dark mirror glass. The house gave the impression that no one lived there. And I recalled the château in the Charente that I had once visited from Angoulême. In front of it, two crazy brothers – one a parliamentarian, the other an architect – had built a replica of the façade of the palace of Versailles, an utterly pointless counterfeit, though one which made a powerful impression from a distance. The windows of that house had been just as gleaming and blind as those of the house we now stood before. Doubtless we should have driven on without accomplishing a thing, if we had not summoned up the nerve, exchanging one of those swift glances, to at least take a look at the garden. Warily we walked round the house. On the north side, where the brickwork was green with damp and variegated ivy partly covered the walls, a mossy path led past the servants' entrance, past a woodshed, on through deep shadows, to emerge, as if upon a stage, onto a terrace with a stone balustrade overlooking a broad, square lawn bordered by flower beds, shrubs and trees. Beyond the lawn, to the west, the grounds opened out into a park landscape studded with lone lime trees, elms and holm oaks, and beyond that lay the gentle undulations of arable land and the white mountains of cloud on the horizon. In silence we gazed at this view, which drew the eye into the distance as it fell and rose in stages, and we looked for a long time, supposing ourselves quite alone, till we noticed a motionless figure lying in the shade cast on the lawn by a lofty cedar in the southwest corner of the garden. It was an old man, his head propped on his arm, and he seemed altogether absorbed in contemplation of the patch of earth immediately before his eyes. We crossed the lawn towards him, every step wonderfully light on the grass. Not till we were almost upon him, though, did he notice us. He stood up, not without a certain embarrassment. Though he was tall and broad-shouldered, he seemed quite stocky, even short. Perhaps this impression came from the way he had of looking, head bowed, over the top of his gold-rimmed reading glasses, a habit which had given him a stooped, almost supplicatory posture. His white hair was combed back, but a few stray wisps kept falling across his strikingly high forehead. I was counting the blades of grass, he said, by way of apology for his absentmindedness. It's a sort of pastime of mine. Rather irritating, I am afraid. He swept back one of his white strands of hair. His movements seemed at once awkward and yet perfectly poised; and there was a similar courtesy, of a style that had long since fallen into disuse, in the way he introduced himself as Dr Henry Selwyn. No doubt, he continued, we had come about the flat. As far as he could say, it had not yet been let, but we should have to wait for Mrs Selwyn's return, since she was the owner of the house and he merely a dweller in the garden, a kind of ornamental hermit. In the course of the conversation that followed these opening remarks, we strolled along the iron railings that marked off the garden from open parkland. We stopped for a moment. Three heavy greys were rounding a little clump of alders, snorting and throwing up clods of turf as they trotted. They took up an expectant position at our side, and Dr Selwyn fed them from his trouser pocket, stroking their muzzles as he did so. I have put them out to grass, he said. I bought them at an auction last year for a few pounds. Otherwise they would doubtless have gone straight to the knacker's yard. They're called Herschel, Humphrey and Hippolytus. I know nothing about their earlier life, but when I bought them they were in a sorry state. Their coats were infested with lice, their eyes were dim, and their hooves were cracked right through from standing in a wet field. But now, said Dr Selwyn, they've made something of a recovery, and they might still have a year or so ahead of them. With that he took his leave of the horses, which were plainly very fond of him, and strolled on with us towards the remoter parts of the garden, pausing now and then and becoming more expansive and circumstantial in his talk. Through the shrubbery on the south side of the lawn, a path led to a walk lined with hazels, where grey squirrels were up to their mischief in the canopy of branches overhead. The

ground was thickly strewn with empty nutshells, and autumn crocuses took the weak light that penetrated the dry, rustling leaves. The hazel walk led to a tennis court bounded by a whitewashed brick wall. Tennis, said Dr Selwyn, used to be my great passion. But now the court has fallen into disrepair, like so much else around here. It's not only the kitchen garden, he continued, indicating the tumble-down Victorian greenhouses and overgrown espaliers, that's on its last legs after years of neglect. More and more, he said, he sensed that

Nature itself was groaning and collapsing beneath the burden we placed upon it. True, the garden, which had originally been meant to supply a large household, and had indeed, by dint of skill and diligence, provided fruit and vegetables for the table throughout the entire year, was still, despite the neglect, producing so much that he had far more than he needed for his own requirements, which admittedly were becoming increasingly modest. Leaving the once well-tended garden to its own devices did have the incidental advantage, said Dr Selwyn, that the things that still grew there, or which he had sown or planted more or less haphazardly, possessed a flavour that he himself found quite exceptionally delicate. We walked between beds of asparagus with the tufts of green at shoulder height, rows of massive artichoke plants, and on to a small group of apple trees, on which there were an abundance of red and yellow apples. Dr Selwyn placed a dozen of these fairy-tale apples, which really did taste better than any I have eaten since, on a rhubarb leaf, and gave them to Clara, remarking that the variety was aptly named Beauty of Bath.

Two days after this first meeting with Dr Selwyn we moved in to Prior's Gate. The previous evening, Mrs Selwyn had shown us the rooms, on the first floor of the east wing, furnished in an idiosyncratic fashion but otherwise pleasant and spacious. We had immediately been very taken with the prospect of spending a few months there, since the view from the high windows across the garden, the park and the massed cloud in the sky was more than ample recompense for the gloomy interior. One only needed to look out, and the gigantic and startlingly ugly sideboard ceased to exist, the mustard yellow paintwork in the kitchen vanished, and the turquoise refrigerator, gas-powered and possibly not without its dangers, seemed to dissolve into nowhere, as if by a miracle. Elli Selwyn was a factory owner's daughter, from Biel in Switzerland, and we soon realized that she had an excellent head for business. She gave us permission to make modest alterations in the flat, to suit our taste. Once the bathroom (which was in an annexe on cast-iron columns and accessible only via a footbridge) had been painted white, she even came up to approve our handiwork. The unfamiliar look prompted her to make the cryptic comment that the bathroom, which had always reminded her of an old-fashioned hothouse, now reminded her of a freshly painted dovecote, an observation that has stuck in my mind to this day as an annihilating verdict on the way we lead our life, though I have not been able to make any change in it. But that is beside the point. Our access to the flat was either by an iron staircase, now painted white as well, that rose from the courtyard to the bathroom footbridge, or (on the ground floor) through a double door into a wide corridor, the walls of which, just below the ceiling, were festooned with a complicated bell-pull system for the summoning of servants. From that passageway one could look into the dark kitchen, where at any hour of the day a female personage of indeterminable age would always be busy at the sink. Elaine, as she was called, wore her hair shorn high up the nape, as the inmates of asylums do. Her facial expressions and movements gave a distraught impression, her lips were always wet, and she was invariably wearing her long grey apron that reached down to her ankles. What work Elaine was doing in the kitchen, day in, day out, remained a mystery to Clara and myself; to the best of our knowledge, no meal, with one single exception, was ever cooked there. Across the corridor, about a foot above the stone floor, there was a door in the wall. Through it, one entered a dark stairwell; and on every floor hidden passageways branched off, running behind walls in such a way that the servants, ceaselessly hurrying to and fro laden with coal scuttles, baskets of firewood, cleaning materials, bed linen and tea trays, never had to cross the paths of their betters. Often I tried to imagine what went on inside the heads of people who led their lives knowing that, behind the walls of the rooms they were in, the shadows of the servants were perpetually flitting past. I fancied they ought to have been afraid of those ghostly creatures who, for scant wages, dealt with the tedious tasks that had to be performed daily. The main access to our rooms was via this rear staircase, at the bottommost level of which, incidentally, was the invariably locked door of Elaine's quarters. This too made us feel somewhat uneasy. Only once did I manage to snatch a glance, and saw that her small room was full of countless dolls, meticulously dressed, most of them wearing something on their heads, standing or sitting around or lying on the bed where Elaine herself slept – if, that is, she ever slept at all, and did not spend the entire night crooning softly as she played with her dolls. On Sundays and holidays we occasionally saw Elaine leaving the house in her Salvation Army uniform. She was often met by a little girl who would then walk beside her, one trusting hand in hers. It took a while for us to grow used to Elaine. What we found particularly unsettling was her intermittent habit, when she was in the kitchen, of breaking into strange, apparently unmotivated, whinnying laughter that would penetrate to the first floor. What was more, Elaine, ourselves excepted, was the sole occupant of the immense house who was always there. Mrs Selwyn was frequently away on her travels for weeks at a time, or was about her business, seeing to the numerous flats she let in town and in nearby villages. As long as the weather permitted, Dr Selwyn liked to be out of doors, and especially in a flint-built hermitage in a remote corner of the garden, which he called his folly and which he had furnished with the essentials. But one morning just a week or so after we had moved in, I saw him standing at an open window of one of his rooms on the west side of the house. He had his spectacles on and was wearing a tartan dressing gown and a white neckerchief.

He was aiming a gun with two inordinately long barrels up into the blue. When at last he fired the shot, after what seemed to me an eternity, the report fell upon the gardens with a shattering crash. Dr Selwyn later explained that he had been finding out whether the gun, which was meant for hunting big game and which he had bought many years ago as a young man, was still in working order after decades of disuse in his dressing room. During that time, as far as he could remember, it had been cleaned and checked over only a couple of times. He told me he had bought the gun when he went to India to take up his first position as a surgeon. At that time, having such a gun was considered obligatory for a man of his caste. He had gone hunting with it only once, though, and had even neglected to put it to inaugural use on that occasion, as he ought to have. So now he had been wondering if the piece still worked, and had established that the recoil alone was enough to kill one.

Otherwise, as I have said, Dr Selwyn was scarcely ever in the house. He lived in his hermitage, giving his entire attention, as he occasionally told me, to thoughts which on the one hand grew vaguer day by day, and, on the other, grew more precise and unambiguous. During our stay in the house he had a visitor only once. It was in the spring, I think, about the end of April, and Elli happened to be away in

Switzerland. One morning Dr Selwyn came up to tell us that he had invited a friend with whom he had been close for many years to dinner and, if it was convenient, he would be delighted if we could make their twosome a *petit comité*. We went down shortly before eight. A fire was blazing against the distinct chill of evening in the vast hearth of the drawing room, which was furnished with a number of four-seater settees and cumbersome armchairs. High on the walls mirrors with blind patches were hung, multiplying the flickering of the firelight and reflecting shifting images. Dr Selwyn was wearing a tie and a tweed jacket with leather patches at the elbows. His friend Edwin Elliott, whom he introduced to us as a well-known botanist and entomologist, was a man of a much slighter build than Dr Selwyn himself, and, while the latter inclined to stoop, he carried himself erect. He too was wearing a tweed jacket. His shirt collar was too large for his scrawny, wrinkled neck, which emerged from it accordion-style, like the neck of certain birds or of a tortoise; his head was small, seeming faintly prehistoric, some kind of throw-back; his eyes, though, shone with sheer wonderful life. At first we talked about my work and our plans for the next year or so, and of the impressions we had, coming from mountainous parts, of England, and particularly of the flat expanse of the county of Norfolk. Dusk fell. Dr Selwyn stood up and, with some ceremony, preceded us into the dining room next door. On the oak table, at which thirty people could have been seated with no difficulty, stood two silver candelabra. Places were set for Dr Selwyn and Edwin at the head and foot of the table, and for Clara and me on the long side facing the windows. By now it was almost dark inside the house, and outside, too, the greenery was thickening with deep, blue shadows. The light of the west still lay on the horizon, though, with mountains of cloud whose snowy formations reminded me of the loftiest alpine massifs, as the night descended. Elaine pushed in a serving trolley equipped with hotplates, some kind of patented design dating from the Thirties. She was wearing her grey full-length apron and went about her work in a silence which she broke only once or twice to mutter something to herself. She lit the candles and shuffled out, as she had come in, without a word. We served ourselves, passing the dishes along the table to one another. The first course consisted of a few pieces of green asparagus covered with marinated leaves of young spinach. The main course was broccoli spears in butter and new potatoes boiled with mint leaves. Dr Selwyn told us that he grew his earlies in the sandy soil of one of the old glasshouses, where they reached the size of walnuts by mid April. The meal was concluded with creamed stewed rhubarb sprinkled with Demarara sugar. Thus almost everything was from the neglected garden. Before we had finished, Edwin turned our conversation to Switzerland, perhaps thinking that Dr Selwyn and I would both have something to say on the subject. And Dr Selwyn did indeed, after a certain hesitation, start to tell us of his stay in Berne shortly before the First World War. In the summer of 1913 (he began), he had completed his medical studies in Cambridge, and had forthwith left for Berne, intending to further his training there. In the event, things had turned out differently, and he had spent most of his time in the Bernese Oberland, taking more and more to mountain climbing. He spent weeks on end in Meiringen, and Oberaar in particular, where he met an alpine guide by the name of Johannes Naegeli, then aged sixty-five, of whom, from the beginning, he was very fond. He went everywhere with Naegeli – up the Zinggenstock, the Scheuchzerhorn and the Rosenhorn, the Lauteraarhorn, the Schreckhorn and the Ewigschneehorn – and never in his life, neither before nor later, did he feel as good as he did then, in the company of that man. When war broke out and I returned to England and was called up, Dr Selwyn said, nothing felt as hard, as I realize now looking back, as saying goodbye to Johannes Naegeli. Even the separation from Elli, whom I had met at Christmas in Berne and married after the war, did not cause me remotely as much pain as the separation from Naegeli. I can still see him standing at the station at Meiringen, waving. But I may

only be imagining it, Dr Selwyn went on in a lower tone, to himself, since Elli has come to seem a stranger to me over the years, whereas Naegeli seems closer whenever he comes to my mind, despite the fact that I never saw him again after that farewell in Meiringen. Not long after mobilization, Naegeli went missing on his way from the Oberaar cabin to Oberaar itself. It was assumed that he had fallen into a crevasse in the Aare glacier. The news reached me in one of the first letters I received when I was in uniform, living in barracks, and it plunged me into a deep depression that nearly led to my being discharged. It was as if I was buried under snow and ice. But this is an old story, said Dr Selwyn after a lengthy pause. We ought really, he said, turning to Edwin, to show our guests the pictures we took on our last visit to Crete. We returned to the drawing room. The logs were glowing in the dark. Dr Selwyn tugged a bell-pull to the right of the fireplace, and almost instantly, as if she had been waiting in the passage for the signal, Elaine pushed in a trolley with a slide projector on it. The large ormolu clock on the mantelpiece and the Meissen figurines, a shepherd and shepherdess and a colourfully clad Moor rolling his eyes, were moved aside, and the wooden-framed screen Elaine had brought in was put up in front of the mirror. The low whirr of the projector began, and the dust in the room, normally invisible, glittered and danced in the beam of light by way of a prelude to the pictures themselves. Their journey to Crete had been made in the springtime. The landscape of the island seemed veiled in bright green as it lay before us. Once or twice, Edwin was to be seen with his field glasses and a container for botanical specimens, or Dr Selwyn in knee-length shorts, with a shoulder bag and butterfly net. One of the shots resembled, even in detail, a photograph of Nabokov in the mountains above Gstaad that I had clipped from a Swiss magazine a few days before.

Strangely enough, both Edwin and Dr Selwyn made a distinctly youthful impression in the pictures they showed us, though at the time they made the trip, exactly ten years earlier, they were already in their late sixties. I sensed that, for both of them, this return of their past selves was an occasion for some emotion. But it may be that it merely seemed that way to me because neither Edwin nor Dr Selwyn was willing or able to make any remark concerning these pictures, whereas they did comment on the many others showing the springtime flora of the island, and all manner of winged and creeping creatures. Whilst their images were on screen, trembling slightly, there was almost total silence in the room. In the last of the pictures we saw the expanse of the Lasithi plateau outspread before us, taken from the heights of one of the northern passes. The shot must have been taken around midday, since the sun was shining into our line of vision. To the south, lofty Mount Spathi, two thousand metres high, towered above the plateau, like a mirage beyond the flood of light. The fields of potatoes and vegetables across the broad valley floor, the orchards and clumps of other trees, and the untilled land, were awash with green upon green, studded with the hundreds of white sails of wind pumps. We sat looking at this picture for a long time in silence too, so long that the glass in the slide shattered and a dark crack fissured across the screen. That view of the Lasithi plateau, held so long till it shattered, made a deep impression on me at the time, yet it later vanished from my mind almost completely. It was not until a few years afterwards that it returned to me, in a London cinema, as I followed a conversation between Kaspar Hauser and his teacher, Daumer, in the kitchen garden at Daumer's home. Kaspar, to the delight of his mentor, was distinguishing for the first time between dream and reality, beginning his account with the words: I was in a dream, and in my dream I saw the Caucasus. The camera then moved from right to left, in a sweeping arc, offering a panoramic view of a plateau ringed by mountains, a plateau with a distinctly Indian look to it, with pagoda-like towers and temples with strange triangular façades amidst the green undergrowth and woodland: follies, in a pulsing dazzle of light, that kept reminding me of the sails of those wind pumps of Lasithi, which in reality I have still not seen to this day.

We moved out of Prior's Gate in mid May 1971. Clara had bought a house one afternoon on the spur of the moment. At first we missed the view, but instead we had the green and grey lancets of two willows at our windows, and even on days when there was no breeze at all they were almost never at rest. The trees were scarcely fifteen metres from the house, and the movement of the leaves seemed so close that at times, when one looked out, one felt a part of it. At fairly regular intervals Dr Selwyn called on us in our as yet almost totally empty house, bringing vegetables and herbs from his garden – yellow and blue beans, carefully scrubbed potatoes, artichokes, chives, sage, chervil and dill. On one of these visits, Clara being away in town, Dr Selwyn and I had a long talk prompted by his asking whether I was ever homesick. I could not think of any adequate reply, but Dr Selwyn, after a pause for thought, confessed (no other word will do) that in recent years he had been beset with homesickness more and more. When I asked where it was that he felt drawn back to, he told me that at the age of seven he had left a village near Grodno in Lithuania with his family. In the late autumn of 1899, his parents, his sisters Gita and Raja, and his Uncle Shani Feldhendler, had ridden to Grodno on a cart that belonged to Aaron Wald the coachman. For years the images of that exodus had been gone from his memory, but recently, he said, they had been returning once again and making their presence felt. I can still see the teacher who taught the children in the *cheder*, where I had been going for two years by then, placing his hand on my parting; I can still see the empty rooms of our house. I see myself sitting topmost on the cart, see the horse's crupper, the vast brown earth, the geese with their outstretched necks in the farmyard mires and the waiting room at Grodno station, overheated by a free-standing railed-off stove, the families of emigrants lying around it. I see the telegraph wires rising and falling past the train window, the façades of the Riga houses, the ship in the docks and the dark corner on deck where we did our best to make ourselves at home in such confined circumstances. The high seas, the trail of smoke, the distant greyness, the lifting and falling of the ship, the fear and hope within us, all of it (Dr Selwyn told me) I can now live through again, as if it were only yesterday. After about a week, far sooner than we had reckoned, we reached our destination. We entered a broad river estuary. Everywhere there were freighters, large and small. Beyond the banks, the land stretched out flat. All the emigrants had gathered on deck and were waiting for the Statue of Liberty to appear out of the drifting mist, since every one of them had booked a passage to Americum, as we called it. When we disembarked we were still in no doubt whatsoever that beneath our feet was the soil of the New World, of the Promised City of New York. But in fact, as we learnt some time later to our dismay (the ship having long since cast off again), we had gone ashore in London. Most of the emigrants, of necessity, adjusted to the situation, but some, in the teeth of all the evidence to the contrary, persisted for a long time in the belief that they were in America. So

I grew up in London, in a basement flat in Whitechapel, in Goulston Street. My father, who was a lens-grinder, used the money he had brought with him to buy a partnership in an optician's business that belonged to a fellow countryman from Grodno by the name of Tosia Feigelis. I went to primary school in Whitechapel and learnt English as if in a dream, because I lapped up, for sheer love, every word from the lips of my beautiful young teacher, Lisa Owen. On my way home from school I would repeat everything she had said that day, over and over, thinking of her as I did so. It was that same beautiful teacher, said Dr Selwyn, who put me in for the Merchant Taylors' School entrance examination. She seemed to take it for granted that I would win one of the scholarships that were available every year to pupils from less well-off homes. And as it turned out I did satisfy her hopes of me; as my Uncle Shani often remarked, the light in the kitchen of our two-room flat in Whitechapel, where I sat up far into the night after my sisters and parents had long since gone to bed, was never off. I learnt and read everything that came my way, and cleared the greatest of obstacles with growing ease. By the end of my school years, when I finished top of my year in the exams, it felt as if I had come a tremendous way. My confidence was at its peak, and in a kind of second confirmation I changed my first name Hersch into Henry, and my surname Seweryn to Selwyn. Oddly enough, I then found that as I began my medical studies (at Cambridge, again with the help of a scholarship) my ability to learn seemed to have slackened, though my examination results were among the best. You already know how things went on from there, said Dr Selwyn: the year in Switzerland, the war, my first year serving in India, and marriage to Elli, from whom

I concealed my true background for a long time. In the Twenties and Thirties we lived in grand style; you have seen for yourself what is left of it. A good deal of Elli's fortune was used up that way. True, I had a practice in town, and was a hospital surgeon, but my income alone would never have permitted us such a life style. In the summer months we would motor right across Europe. Next to tennis, said Dr Selwyn, motoring was my great passion in those days. The cars are all still in the garage, and they may be worth something by now. But I have never been able to bring myself to sell anything, except perhaps, at one point, my soul. People have told me repeatedly that I haven't the slightest sense of money. I didn't even have the foresight, he said, to provide for my old age by paying into a pension scheme. That is why I am now practically a pauper. Elli, on the other hand, has made good use of the not inconsiderable remainder of her fortune, and now she must no doubt be a wealthy woman. I still don't know for sure what made us drift apart, the money or revealing the secret of my origins, or simply the decline of love. The years of the second war, and the decades after, were a blinding, bad time for me, about which I could not say a thing even if I wanted to. In 1960, when I had to give up my practice and my patients, I severed my last ties with what they call the real world. Since then, almost my only companions have been plants and animals. Somehow or other I seem to get on well with them, said Dr Selwyn with an inscrutable smile, and, rising, he made a gesture that was most unusual for him. He offered me his hand in farewell.

After that call, Dr Selwyn's visits to us became fewer and further between. The last time we saw him was the day he brought Clara a bunch of white roses with twines of honeysuckle, shortly before we left for a holiday in France. A few weeks after, late that summer, he took his own life with a bullet from his heavy hunting rifle. He had sat on the edge of his bed (we learnt on our return from France) with the gun between his legs, placed the muzzle of the rifle at his jaw, and then, for the first time since he bought the gun before

MERCREDI 23 JUILLET 1986

2 3 JUIL. 1986

Trois fois coup sur coup dans les Alpes

CH/FD/ Morts suspectes

Des linceuls s'

Hier, on a identifié le cadavre d'un guide disparu en 1914

Mais le phénomène des glaces qui rendent leurs victimes e

Septante-deux ans après sa mort, le corps du guide bernois Johannes Naegeli a été libéré de son linceul de glace.

PAR Véronique TISSIÈRES

Hier, on apprenait en effet que la dépouille découverte jeudi dernier sur le glacier supérieur de l'Aar était celle de cet homme de Willingen (près de Meiringen) dont on avait perdu la trace depuis ces jours d'été 1914, où il resta seul à la cabane du CAS. Agé, à l'époque de 66 ans, il est probable qu'il tenta de regagner la plaine par le glacier ; il n'y parvint jamais et toutes les recherches entreprises à l'époque demeurèrent sans résultats.

Coïncidence ? Quelque jours avant la découverte de la dépouille du guide bernois, le corps d'un fantassin de l'armée austro-hongroise, victime de la Première Guerre mondiale, émergeait du Giogo Lungo (Dolomites). Début juillet, enfin, la Vallée-Blanche rendait le cadavre d'une de ses victimes...

Trois cas recensés dans le massif alpin au cours des quinze premiers jours de juillet ! C'est beaucoup, c'
même tout à fait exceptionnel, car
restitution de corps par les glacie
contrairement à ce que pourraient la
ser supposer les exemples ci-dess
reste un phénomène rare. « Rare m
cyclique, précise-t-on au service
secours en haute montagne de la pol
valaisanne. Il ne faut en effet pas p
dre de vue que ces restitutions s
étroitement liées au mouvement
masses de glace. Certaines années,
glaciers du canton livrent deux vic
mes presque coup sur coup, puis p
rien pendant longtemps. »

Ce fut le cas l'an dernier. Le co
d'une jeune femme, disparue qua
ans auparavant, fut retrouvé à la s
face du glacier de Breney (val
Bagnes). Peu après, le Théodule ren

LE GLACIER DE L'AAR
Qui vient de rendre un guide décédé en 1914.

L'hist

Film, légendes, la rest
l'imagination. Mais il

C'était en 1937. Fin août, la s
son terminée, le gardien de
cabane Bertol (au-dessus d'Aro
quitta la petite bâtisse pour la
lée. Il n'y arriva jamais. Des rech
ches furent entreprises, en vain.

Qu'était-il devenu ? Les lang
allèrent bon train dans la région.
jasa, on parla d'une escapade
Italie. D'autant plus qu'il n'avait
disparu seul, mais avec la ca
contenant les recettes du refu
Pas une grosse somme, de q
toutefois recommencer une n
velle vie ailleurs.

Sept ans plus tard, un gu
repère, émergeant de la masse
glacier, une main tenant fermem

departing for India, had fired a shot with intent to kill. When we received the news, I had no great difficulty in overcoming the initial shock. But certain things, as I am increasingly becoming aware, have a way of returning unexpectedly, often after a lengthy absence. In late July 1986 I was in Switzerland for a few days. On the morning of the 23rd I took the train from Zurich to Lausanne. As the train slowed to cross the Aare bridge, approaching Berne, I gazed way beyond the city to the mountains of the Oberland. At that point, as I recall, or perhaps merely imagine, the memory of Dr Selwyn returned to me for the first time in a long while. Three quarters of an hour later, not wanting to miss the landscape around Lake Geneva, which never fails to astound me as it opens out, I was just laying aside a Lausanne paper I'd bought in Zurich when my eye was caught by a report that said the remains of the Bernese alpine guide Johannes Naegeli, missing since summer 1914, had been released by the Oberaar glacier, seventy-two years later. And so they are ever returning to us, the dead. At times they come back from the ice more than seven decades later and are found at the edge of the moraine, a few polished bones and a pair of hobnailed boots.

PAUL BEREYTER

There is mist that no eye can dispel

In January 1984, the news reached me from S that on the evening of the 30th of December, a week after his seventy-fourth birthday, Paul Bereyter, who had been my teacher at primary school, had put an end to his life. A short distance from S, where the railway track curves out of a willow copse into the open fields, he had lain himself down in front of a train. The obituary in the local paper was headed "Grief at the Loss of a Popular Teacher" and there was no mention of the fact that Paul Bereyter had died of his own free will, or through a self-destructive compulsion. It spoke merely of the dead man's services to education, his dedicated care for his pupils, far beyond the call of duty, his great love of music, his astonishing inventiveness, and of much else in the same vein. Almost by way of an aside, the obituary added, with no further explanation, that during the Third Reich Paul Bereyter had been prevented from practising his chosen profession. It was this curiously unconnected, inconsequential statement, as much as the violent manner of his death, which led me in the years that followed to think more and more about Paul Bereyter, until, in the end, I had to get beyond my own very fond memories of him and discover the story I did not know. My investigations took me back to S, which I had visited less and less since leaving school. I soon learned that, right up to his death, Paul Bereyter had rented rooms there, in a house built in 1970 on the land that had once been Dagobert Lerchenmüller's nursery and market garden, but he had seldom lived there, and it was thought that he was mostly abroad, no one quite knew where. His continual absence from the town, and his increasingly odd behaviour, which had first become apparent a few years before his retirement, gave him the reputation of an eccentric. This reputation, regardless of his undoubted pedagogic ability, had clung to Paul Bereyter for some considerable time, and had, as far as his death was concerned, confirmed the belief among the people of S (amidst whom Paul Bereyter had grown up and, albeit it with certain interruptions, always lived) that things had happened as they were bound to happen. The few conversations I had in S with people who had known Paul Bereyter were not very revealing, and the only thing that seemed remarkable was that no one called him Paul Bereyter or even Bereyter the teacher. Instead, he was invariably referred to simply as Paul, giving me the impression that in the eyes of his contemporaries he had never really grown up. I was reminded then of how we had only ever spoken of him as Paul at school, not without respect but rather as one might refer to an exemplary older brother, and in a way this implied that he was one of us, or that we belonged together. This, as I have come to realize, was merely a fabrication of our minds, because, even though Paul knew and understood us, we, for our part, had little idea of what he was or what went on inside him. And so, belatedly, I tried to get closer to him, to imagine what his life was like in that spacious apartment on the top floor of Lerchenmüller's old house, which had once stood where the present block of flats is now, amidst an array of green vegetable patches and colourful flower beds, in the gardens where Paul often helped out of an afternoon. I imagined him lying in the open air on his balcony where he would often sleep in the summer, his face canopied by the hosts of the stars. I imagined him skating in winter, alone on the fish ponds at Moosbach; and I imagined him stretched out on the track. As I pictured him, he had taken off his spectacles and put them on the ballast stones by his side. The gleaming bands of steel, the crossbars of the sleepers, the spruce trees on the hillside above the village of Altstädten, the arc of the mountains he knew so well, were a blur before his short-sighted eyes, smudged out in the gathering dusk. At the last, as the thunderous sound approached, all he saw was a darkening greyness and, in the midst of it, needle-sharp, the snow-white silhouettes of three mountains: the Kratzer, the Trettach and the Himmelsschrofen. Such endeavours to imagine his life and death did not, as I had to admit, bring me any closer to Paul, except at best for brief emotional moments of the kind that seemed presumptuous to me. It is in order to avoid this sort of wrongful trespass that I have written down what I know of Paul Bereyter.

In December 1952 my family moved from the village of W to the small town of S, 19 kilometres away. The journey – during which I gazed out of the cab of Alpenvogel's wine-red furniture van at the endless lines of trees along the roadsides, thickly frosted over and appearing before us out of the lightless morning mist – seemed like a voyage halfway round the world, though it will have lasted an hour at the very most. When at length we trundled across the Ach bridge into S, at that time no more than a small market town of perhaps nine thousand souls, I was overcome by a powerful feeling that a new life filled with the bustle of cities would be starting for us there. The blue enamel street names, the huge clock in front of the old railway station, and what seemed to me then the truly magnificent façade of the Wittelsbacher Hof Hotel, were all, I felt, unmistakable signs of a new beginning. It was, I thought, particularly auspicious that the rows of houses were interrupted here and there by patches of waste land on which stood ruined buildings, for ever since I had once visited Munich I had felt nothing to be so unambiguously linked to the word *city* as the presence of heaps of rubble, fire-scorched walls, and the gaps of windows through which one could see the vacant air.

On the afternoon that we arrived, the temperature plummeted. A snow blizzard set in that continued for the rest of the day and eased off to an even, calm snowfall only towards the night. When I went to the school in S for the first time the following morning, the snow lay so thick that I felt a kind of exhilaration at the sight of it. The class I joined was the third grade, which was taught by Paul Bereyter. There I stood, in my dark green pullover with the leaping stag on it, in front of fifty-one fellow pupils, all staring at me with the greatest possible curiosity, and, as if from a great distance, I heard Paul say that I had arrived at precisely the right moment, since he had been telling the story of the stag's leap only the day before, and now the image of the leaping stag, worked into the fabric of my pullover, could be copied onto the blackboard. He asked me to take off the pullover and take a seat in the back row beside Fritz Binswanger for the time being, while he, using my picture of a leaping stag, would show us how an image could be broken down into numerous tiny pieces – small crosses, squares or dots – or else assembled from these. In no time I was bent over my exercise book, beside Fritz, copying the leaping stag from the blackboard onto my grid-marked paper. Fritz too, who (as I soon learnt) was repeating his third grade year, was taking visible pains over his effort, yet his progress was infinitely slow. Even when those who had started late were long finished, he still had little more than a dozen crosses on his page. We exchanged silent glances, and I rapidly completed his fragmentary piece of work. From that day on, in the almost two years that we sat next to each other, I did most of his arithmetic, his writing and his drawing exercises. It was very easy to do, and to do seamlessly, as it were, chiefly because Fritz and I had the self-same, incorrigibly sloppy handwriting (as Paul repeatedly observed, shaking his head), with the one difference that Fritz could not write quickly and I could not write slowly. Paul had no objection to our working together; indeed, to encourage us further he hung the case of cockchafers on the wall beside our desk. It had a deep frame and was half-filled with soil. In it, as well as a pair of cockchafers labelled Melolontha vulgaris in the old German hand, there were a clutch of eggs, a pupa and a larva, and, in the upper portion, cockchafers were hatching, flying, and eating the leaves of apple trees. That case, demonstrating the mysterious metamorphosis of the cockchafer, inspired Fritz and me in the late spring to an intensive study of the whole nature of cockchafers, including anatomical examination and culminating in the cooking and eating of a cockchafer stew. Fritz, in fact, who came from a large family of farm labourers at Schwarzenbach and, as far as was known, had never had a real father, took the liveliest interest in anything connected with food, its preparation, and the eating of it. Every day he would expatiate in great detail on the quality of the sandwiches I brought with me and shared with him, and on our way home from school we would always stop to look in the window of Turra's delicatessen, or to look at the display at Einsiedler's exotic fruit emporium, where the main attraction was a dark green trout aquarium with air bubbling up through the water. On one occasion when we had been standing for a long time outside Einsiedler's, from the shadowy interior of which a pleasant coolness wafted out that September noon, old Einsiedler himself appeared in the doorway and made each of us a present of a white butterpear. This constituted a veritable miracle, not only because the fruits were such splendid rarities but chiefly because Einsiedler was widely known to be of a choleric disposition, a man who despised nothing so much as serving the few customers he still had. It was while he was eating the white butterpear that Fritz confided to me that he planned to be a chef; and he did indeed become a chef, one who could be said without exaggeration to enjoy international renown. He perfected his culinary skills at the Grand Hotel Dolder in Zurich and the Victoria Jungfrau in Interlaken, and was subsequently as much in demand in New York as in Madrid or London. It was when he was in London that we met again, one April morning in 1984, in the reading room of the British Museum, where I was researching the history of Bering's Alaska expedition and Fritz was studying eighteenth-century French cookbooks. By chance we were sitting just one aisle apart, and when we both happened to look up from our work at the same moment we immediately recognized each other despite the quarter century that had passed. In the cafeteria we told each other the stories of our lives, and talked for a long time about Paul, of whom Fritz mainly recalled that he had never once seen him eat.

In our classroom, the plan of which we had to draw to scale in our exercise books, there were twenty-six desks screwed fast to the oiled floorboards.

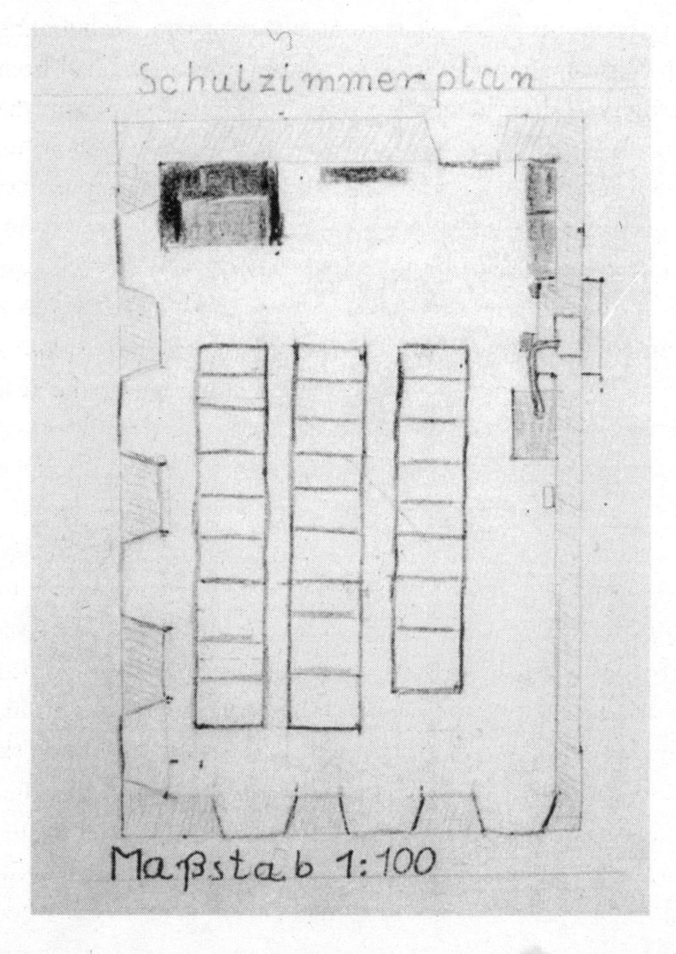

From the raised teacher's desk, behind which the crucifix hung on the wall, one could look down on the pupils' heads, but I cannot remember Paul ever occupying that elevated position. If he was not at the blackboard or at the cracked oilcloth map of the world, he would walk down the rows of desks, or lean, arms folded, against the cupboard beside the green tiled stove. His favourite place, though, was by one of the south-facing windows let into deep bays in the wall. Outside those windows, from amidst the branches of the old apple orchard at Frey's distillery, starlings' nesting boxes on long wooden poles reached into the sky, which was bounded in the distance by the jagged line of the Lech valley Alps, white with snow for almost the entire school year. The teacher who preceded Paul, Hormayr, who had been feared for his pitiless regime and would have offenders kneel for hours on sharp-edged blocks of wood, had had the windows half whitewashed so that the children could not see out. The first thing Paul did when he took up the job in 1946 was to remove the whitewash, painstakingly scratching it away with a razor blade, a task which was, in truth, not urgent, since Paul was in any case in the habit of opening the windows wide, even when the weather was bad, indeed even in the harshest cold of winter, being firmly convinced that lack of oxygen impaired the capacity to think. What he liked most, then, was to stand in one of the window bays towards the head of the room, half facing the class and half turned to look out, his face at a slightly upturned angle with the sunlight glinting on his glasses; and from that position on the periphery he would talk across to us. In well-structured sentences, he spoke without any touch of dialect but with a slight impediment of speech or timbre, as if the sound were coming not from the larynx but from somewhere near the heart. This sometimes gave one the feeling that it was all being powered by clockwork inside him and Paul in his entirety was a mechanical human made of tin and other metal parts, and might be put out of operation for ever by the smallest functional hitch. He would run his left hand through his hair as he spoke, so that it stood on end, dramatically emphasizing what he said. Not infrequently he would also take out his handkerchief, and, in anger at what he considered (perhaps not unjustly) our wilful stupidity, bite on it. After bizarre turns of this kind he would always take off his glasses and stand unseeing and defenceless in the midst of the class, breathing on the lenses and polishing them with such assiduity that it seemed he was glad not to have to see us for a while.

Paul's teaching did include the curriculum then laid down for primary schools: the multiplication tables, basic arithmetic, German and Latin handwriting, nature study, the history and customs of our valley, singing, and what was known as physical education. Religious studies, however, were not taught by Paul himself; instead, once a week, we first had Catechist Meier (spelt e-i), who lisped, and then Beneficiary Meyer (spelt e-y), who spoke in a booming voice, to teach us the meaning of sin and confession, the creed, the church calendar, the seven deadly sins, and more of a similar kind. Paul, who was rumoured to be a free-thinker, something I long found incomprehensible, always contrived to avoid Meier-with-an-i or Meyer-with-a-y both at the beginning and at the end of their religion lessons, for there was plainly nothing he found quite so repellent as Catholic sanctimoniousness. And when he returned to the classroom after these lessons to find an Advent altar chalked on the blackboard in purple, or a red and yellow monstrance, or other such things, he would instantly rub out the offending works of art with a conspicuous vigour and thoroughness. Always before our religion lessons, Paul would always top up to the brim the holy water stoup, embellished with a flaming Sacred Heart, that was fixed by the door, using (I often saw him do it) the watering can with which he normally watered the geraniums. Because of this, the Beneficiary never managed to put the holy water bottle he always carried in his shiny black pigskin briefcase to use. He did not dare simply to tip out the water from the brimful stoup, and so, in his endeavour to account for the seemingly inexhaustible Sacred Heart, he was torn between his suspicion that systematic malice was involved and the intermittent hope that this was a sign from a Higher Place, perhaps indeed a miracle. Most assuredly, though, both the Beneficiary and the Catechist considered Paul a lost soul, for we were called upon more than once to pray for our teacher to convert to the true faith. Paul's aversion to the Church of Rome was far more than a mere question of principle, though; he genuinely had a horror of God's vicars and the mothball smell they gave off. He not only did not attend church on Sundays, but purposely left town, going as far as he could into the mountains, where he no longer heard the bells. If the weather was not good he would spend his Sunday mornings together with Colo the cobbler, who was a philosopher and a downright atheist who took the Lord's day, if he was not playing chess with Paul, as the occasion to work on pamphlets and tracts against the one True Church. Once (I now remember) I witnessed a moment when Paul's aversion to hypocrisy of any description won an incontestable victory over the forbearance with which he generally endured the intellectual infirmities of the world he lived in. In the class above me there was a pupil by the name of Ewald Reise who had fallen completely under the Catechist's influence and displayed a degree of overdone piety – it would not be unfair to say, ostentatiously – quite incredible in a ten-year-old. Even at this tender age, Ewald Reise already looked like a fully-fledged chaplain. He was the only boy in the whole school who wore a coat, complete with a purple scarf folded over at his chest and held in place with a large safety pin. Reise, whose head was never uncovered (even in the heat of summer he wore a straw hat or a light linen cap), struck Paul so powerfully as an example of the stupidity, both inbred and wilfully acquired, that he so detested, that one day when the boy forgot to doff his hat to him in the street Paul removed the hat for him, clipped his ear, and then replaced the hat on Reise's head with the rebuke that even a prospective chaplain should greet his teacher with politeness when they met.

Paul spent at least a quarter of all his lessons on teaching us things that were not on the syllabus. He taught us the rudiments of algebra, and his enthusiasm for natural history once led him (to the horror of his neighbours) to boil the flesh off a dead fox he had found in the woods, in an old preserving pan on his kitchen stove, so that he would then be able to reassemble the skeleton with us in school. We never read the text books that were intended for third and fourth years at primary school, as Paul found them ridiculous and hypocritical; instead, our reading was almost exclusively the *Rheinische Hausfreund*, a collection of tales for the home, sixty copies of which Paul had procured, I suspect at his own expense. Many of the stories in it, such as the one about a decapitation performed in secret, made the most vivid impression on me, and those impressions have not faded to this day; more than anything else (why, I cannot say) I clearly recall the words said by the passing pilgrim to the woman who kept the Baselstab Inn: When I return, I shall bring you a sacred cockleshell from the Strand at Askalon, or a rose from Jericho. – At least once a week, Paul taught us French. He began with the simple observation that he had once lived in France, that people there spoke French, that he knew how to do it, and that we could easily do it too, if we wished. One May morning we sat outside in the school yard, and on that fresh bright day we easily grasped what *un beau jour* meant, and that a chestnut tree in blossom might just as well be called *un chataignier en fleurs.* Indeed, Paul's teaching was altogether the most lucid, in general, that one could imagine. On principle he placed the greatest value on taking us out of the school building whenever the opportunity arose and observing as much as we could around the town – the electric power station with the transformer plant, the smelting furnaces and the steam-powered forge at the iron foundry, the basketware workshops, and the cheese dairy. We visited the mash room at the brewery, and the malt house, where the silence was so total that none of us dared to say a word. And one day we visited Corradi the gunsmith, who had been practising his trade in S for close on sixty years. Corradi invariably wore a green eyeshade and, whenever the light that came through his workshop window permitted, he would be bent over the complicated locks of old fire-arms which no one but himself, far and wide, could repair. When he had succeeded in fixing a lock, he would go out into the front garden with the gun and fire a few rounds into the air for sheer pleasure, to mark the end of the job.

What Paul termed his "object lessons" took us, in the course of time, to all of the nearby locations that were of interest for one reason or another and could be reached on foot within about two hours. We visited Fluhenstein Castle, explored the Starzlach Gorge, went to the conduit house above Hofen and the powder magazine where the Veterans' Association kept their ceremonial cannon, on the hill where the stations of the cross led up to the Calvary Chapel. We were more than a little surprised when, after various preliminary studies that took several weeks, we succeeded in finding the derelict tunnel of the brown coal mine on the Straussberg, which had been abandoned after the First

World War, with what was left of the cable railway that had transported the coal from the mouth of the tunnel to the station at Altstädten below. Not all our excursions, however, were made with a specific purpose. On particularly fine days we often simply went out into the fields, to go on with our botany or sometimes, under a botanical pretext, simply to idle the time away. On these occasions, usually in early summer, the son of Wohlfahrt the barber and undertaker would frequently join us. Known to everyone as Mangold, and reckoned to be not quite right in the head, he was of uncertain age and of a childlike disposition. It made him deliriously happy, a gangling fellow among school-children not yet into adolescence, to tell us on which day of the week any past or future date we cared to name would fall – despite the fact that he was otherwise incapable of solving the simplest mathematical problem. If, say, one told Mangold that one was born on the 18th of May, 1944, he would shoot back without a moment's hesitation that that was a Thursday. And if one tried difficult questions on him, such as the Pope's or King Ludwig's date of birth, again he could say what day of the week it was, in a flash. Paul, who excelled at mental arithmetic and was a first-rate mathematician, tried for years to fathom Mangold's secret, setting him complicated tests, asking questions, and going to a variety of other lengths. As far as I am aware, though, neither he nor anyone else ever worked it out, because Mangold hardly understood the questions he was asked. That aside, Paul, like Mangold and the rest of us, clearly enjoyed our outings into the country-side. Wearing his windcheater, or simply in shirtsleeves, he would walk ahead of us with his face slightly upturned, taking those long and springy steps that were so characteristic, the very image (as I realize only now as I look back) of the German *Wandervogel* hiking movement, which must have had a lasting influence on him from his youth. Paul was in the habit of whistling continuously as he walked across the fields. He was an amazingly good whistler; the sound he produced was marvellously rich, exactly like a flute's. And even when he was climbing a mountain, he would with apparent ease whistle whole runs and ties in connected sequence, not just anything, but fine, thoroughly composed passages and melodies that none of us had ever heard before, and which infallibly gave a wrench to my heart whenever, years later, I rediscovered them in a Bellini opera or Brahms sonata. When we rested on the way, Paul would take his clarinet, which he carried with him without fail in an old cotton stocking, and play various pieces, chiefly slow movements, from the classical repertoire, with which I was then completely unfamiliar. Apart from these music lessons at which we were merely required to provide an audience, we would learn a new song at least once a fortnight, the contemplative again being given preference over the merry. "Zu Strassburg auf der Schanz, da fing mein Trauern an", "Auf den Bergen die Burgen", "Im Krug zum grünen Kranze" or "Wir gleiten hinunter das Ufer entlang" were the kinds of songs we learnt. But I did not grasp the true meaning that music had for Paul till the extremely talented son of Brandeis the organist, who was already studying at the conservatoire, came to our singing lesson (at Paul's instigation, I assume) and played on his violin to an audience of peasant boys (for that is what we were, almost without exception). Paul, who was standing by the window as usual, far from being able to hide the emotion that young Brandeis's playing produced in him, had to remove his glasses because his eyes had filled with tears. As I remember it, he even turned away in order to conceal from us the sob that rose in him. It was not only music, though, that affected Paul in this way; indeed, at any time – in the middle of a lesson, at break, or on one of our outings – he might stop or sit down somewhere, alone and apart from us all, as if he, who was always in good spirits and seemed so cheerful, was in fact desolation itself.

It was not until I was able to fit my own fragmentary recollections into what Lucy Landau told me that I was able to understand that desolation even in part. It was Lucy Landau, as I found out in the course of my enquiries in S, who had arranged for Paul to be buried in the churchyard there. She lived at Yverdon, and it was there, on a summer's day in the second year after Paul died, a day I recall as curiously soundless, that I paid her the first of several visits. She began by telling me that at the age of seven, together with her father, who was an art historian and a widower, she had left her home town of Frankfurt. The modest lakeside villa in which she lived had been built by a chocolate manufacturer at the turn of the century, for his old age. Mme Landau's father had bought it in the summer of 1933 despite the fact that the purchase, as Mme Landau put it, ate up almost his whole fortune, with the result that she spent her entire childhood and the war years that followed in a house well-nigh unfurnished. Living in those empty rooms had never struck her as a deprivation, though; rather, it had seemed, in a way not easy to describe, to be a special favour or distinction conferred upon her by a happy turn of events. For instance, she remembered her eighth birthday very clearly. Her father had spread a white paper cloth on a table on the terrace, and there she and Ernest, her new school friend, had sat at dinner while her father, wearing a black waistcoat and with a napkin over his forearm, had played the waiter, to rare perfection.

At that time, the empty house with its wide-open windows and the trees about it softly swaying was her backdrop for a magical theatre show. And then, Mme Landau continued, bonfire after bonfire began to burn along the lakeside as far as St Aubin and beyond, and she was completely convinced that all of it was being done purely for her, in honour of her birthday. Ernest, said Mme Landau with a smile that was meant for him, across the years that had intervened, Ernest knew of course that the bonfires that glowed brightly in the darkness all around were burning because it was Swiss National Day, but he most tactfully forbore to spoil my bliss with explanations of any kind. Indeed, the discretion of Ernest, who was the youngest of a large family, has always remained exemplary to my way of thinking, and no one ever equalled him, with the possible exception of Paul, whom I unfortunately met far too late – in summer 1971 at Salins-les-Bains in the French Jura.

A lengthy silence followed this disclosure before Mme Landau added that she had been reading Nabokov's autobiography on a park bench on the Promenade des Cordeliers when Paul, after walking by her twice, commented on her reading, with a courtesy that bordered on the extravagant. From then on, all that afternoon and throughout the weeks that followed, he had made the most appealing conversation, in his somewhat old-fashioned but absolutely correct French. He had explained to her at the outset, by way of introduction, as it were, that he had come to Salins-les-Bains, which he knew of old, because what he referred to as his condition had been deteriorating in recent years to the point where his claustrophobia made him unable to teach and he saw his pupils, although he had always felt affection for them (he stressed this), as contemptible and repulsive creatures, the very sight of whom had prompted an utterly groundless violence in him on more than one occasion. Paul did his best to conceal his distress and the fear of insanity that came out in confessions of this kind. Thus, Mme Landau said, he had told her, only a few days after they had met, with an irony that made everything seem light and unimportant, of his recent attempt to take his own life. He described this episode as an embarrassment of the first order which he was loath to recall but about which he felt obliged to tell her so that she would know all that was needful concerning the strange companion at whose side she was so kind as to be walking about summery Salins. Le pauvre Paul, said Mme Landau, lost in thought, and then, looking across at me once more, observed that in her long life she had known quite a number of men – closely, she emphasized, a mocking expression on her face – all of whom, in one way or another, had been enamoured of themselves. Every one of these gentlemen, whose names, mercifully, she had mostly forgotten, had, in the end, proved to be an insensitive boor, whereas Paul, who was almost consumed by the loneliness within him, was the most considerate and entertaining companion one could wish for. The two of them, said Mme Landau, took delightful walks in Salins, and made excursions out of town. They visited the thermal baths and the salt galleries together, and spent whole afternoons up at Fort Belin. They gazed down from the bridges into the green water of the Furieuse, telling each other stories as they stood there. They went to the house at Arbois where Pasteur grew up, and in Arc-et-Senans they had seen the saltern buildings which in the eighteenth century had been constructed as an ideal model for factory, town and society; on this occasion,

Paul, in a conjecture she felt to be most daring, had linked the bourgeois concept of Utopia and order, as expressed in the designs and buildings of Nicolas Ledoux, with the progressive destruction of natural life. She was surprised, as she talked about it now, said Mme Landau, at how clear the images that she had supposed buried beneath grief at the loss of Paul still were to her. Clearest of all, though, were the memories of their outing – a somewhat laborious business despite the chair lift – up Montrond, from the summit of which she had gazed down for an eternity at Lake Geneva and the surrounding country, which looked considerably reduced in size, as if intended for a model railway. The tiny features below, taken together with the gentle mass of Montblanc towering above them, the Vanoise glacier almost invisible in the shimmering distance, and the Alpine panorama that occupied half the horizon, had for the first time in her life awoken in her a sense of the contrarieties that are in our longings.

On a later visit to the Villa Bonlieu, when I enquired further about Paul's apparent familiarity with the French Jura and the area around Salins from an earlier time in his life, which Mme Landau had intimated, I learnt that in the period from autumn 1935 to early 1939 he had first been for a short while in Besançon and had then taught as house tutor to a family by the name of Passagrain in Dôle. As if in explanation of this fact, not at first glance compatible with the circumstances of a German primary school teacher in the Thirties, Mme Landau put before me a large album which contained photographs documenting not only the period in question but indeed, a few gaps aside, almost the whole of Paul Bereyter's life, with notes penned in his own hand. Again and again, from front to back and from back to front, I leafed through the album that afternoon, and since then I have returned to it time and again, because, looking at the pictures in it, it truly seemed to me, and still does, as if the dead were coming back, or as if we were on the point of joining them. The earliest photographs told the story of a happy childhood in the Bereyter family home in Blumenstrasse, right next to Lerchenmüller's nursery garden, and frequently showed Paul with his cat or with a rooster that was evidently completely domesticated. The years in a country boarding school followed, scarcely any less happy than the years of childhood that had gone before, and then Paul's entry into teacher training college at Lauingen, which he referred to as

the teacher processing factory in his gloss. Mme Landau observed that Paul had submitted to this training, which followed the most narrow-minded of guidelines and was dictated by a morbid Catholicism, only because he wanted to teach children at whatever cost – even if it meant enduring training of that kind. Only because he was so absolute and unconditional an idealist had he been able to survive his time at Lauingen without his soul being harmed in any way. In 1934 to 1935, Paul, then aged twenty-four, did his probation year at the primary school in S, teaching, as I learnt to my amazement, in the very classroom where a good fifteen years later he taught a pack of children scarcely distinguishable

from those pictured here, a class that included myself. The summer of 1935, which followed his probation year, was one of the finest times of all (as the photographs and Mme Landau's comments made clear) in the life of prospective primary school teacher Paul Bereyter. That summer, Helen Hollaender from Vienna spent several weeks in S. Helen,

who was a month or so older, spent that time at the Bereyter home, a fact which is glossed in the album with a double exclamation mark, while her mother put up at Pension Luitpold for the duration. Helen, so Mme Landau believed, came as a veritable revelation to Paul; for if these pictures can be trusted, she said, Helen Hollaender was an independent-spirited, clever woman, and furthermore her waters ran deep. And in those waters Paul liked to see his own reflection.

And now, continued Mme Landau, just think: early that September, Helen returned with her mother to Vienna, and Paul took up his first teaching post in the remote village of W. There, before he had had the time to do more than remember the children's names, he was served official notice that it would not be possible for him to remain as a teacher, because of the new laws, with which he was no doubt familiar. The wonderful future he had dreamt of that summer collapsed without a sound like the proverbial house of cards. All his prospects blurred. For the first time, he experienced that insuperable sense of defeat that was so often to beset him in later times and which, finally, he could not shake off. At the end of October, said Mme Landau, drawing to a close for the time being, Paul travelled via Basle to Besançon, where he took a position as a house tutor that had been found for him through a business associate of his father. How wretched he must have felt at that time is apparent in a small photograph taken one Sunday afternoon, which shows Paul on the left, a Paul who had plunged within a month

from happiness to misfortune, and was so terribly thin that he seems almost to have reached a physical vanishing point. Mme Landau could not tell me exactly what became of Helen Hollaender. Paul had preserved a resolute silence on the subject, possibly because he was plagued by a sense of having failed her or let her down. As far as Mme Landau had been able to discover, there could be little doubt that Helen and her mother had been deported, in one of those special trains that left Vienna at dawn, probably to Theresienstadt in the first instance.

Gradually, Paul Bereyter's life began to emerge from the background. Mme Landau was not in the least surprised that I was unaware, despite the fact that I came from S and knew what the town was like, that old Bereyter was what was termed half Jewish, and Paul, in consequence, only three quarters an Aryan. Do you know, she said on one of my visits to Yverdon, the systematic thoroughness with which these people kept silent in the years after the war, kept their secrets, and even, I sometimes think, really did forget, is nothing more than the other side of the perfidious way in which Schöferle, who ran a coffee house in S, informed Paul's mother Thekla, who had been on stage for some time in Nuremberg, that the presence of a lady who was married to a half Jew might be embarrassing to his respectable clientele, and begged to request her, with respect of course, not to take her afternoon coffee at his house any more. I do not find it surprising, said Mme Landau, not in the slightest, that you were unaware of the meanness and treachery that a family like the Bereyters were exposed to in a miserable hole such as S then was, and such as it still is despite all the so-called progress; it does not surprise me at all, since that is inherent in the logic of the whole wretched sequence of events.

In an effort to resume a more factual tone after the little outburst she had permitted herself, Mme Landau told me that Paul's father, a man of refinement and inclined to melancholy, came from Gunzenhausen in Franconia, where Paul's grandfather Amschel Bereyter had a junk shop and had married his Christian maid, who had grown very fond of him after a few years of service in his house. At that time Amschel was already past fifty, while Rosina was still in her mid twenties. Their marriage, which was naturally a rather quiet one, produced only one child, Theodor, the father of Paul. After an apprenticeship in Augsburg as a salesman, Theodor was employed for a lengthy spell in a Nuremberg department store, working his way up to the higher echelons, before moving to S in 1900 to open an emporium with capital saved partly from his earnings and partly borrowed. He sold everything in the emporium, from coffee to collar studs, camisoles to cuckoo clocks, candied sugar to collapsible top hats. Paul once described that wonderful emporium to her in detail, said Mme Landau, when he was in hospital in Berne in 1975, his eyes bandaged after an operation for cataracts. He said that he could see things then with the greatest clarity, as one sees them in dreams, things he had not thought he still had within him. In his childhood, everything in the emporium seemed far too high up for him, doubtless because he himself was small, but also because the shelves reached all the four metres up to the ceiling. The light in the emporium, coming through the small transom windows let into the tops of the display window backboards, was dim even on the brightest of days, and it must have seemed all the murkier to him as a child, Paul had said, as he moved on his tricycle, mostly on the lowest level, through the ravines between tables, boxes and counters, amidst a variety of smells – mothballs and lily-of-the-valley soap were always the most pungent, while felted wool and loden cloth assailed the nose only in wet weather, herrings and linseed oil in hot. For hours on end, Paul had said, deeply moved by his own memories, he had ridden in those days past the dark rows of bolts of material, the gleaming leather boots, the preserve jars, the galvanized watering cans, the whip stand, and the case that had seemed especially magical to him, in which rolls of Gütermann's sewing thread were neatly arrayed behind little glass windows, in every colour of the rainbow. The emporium staff consisted of Frommknecht, the clerk and accountant, one of whose shoulders was permanently raised higher from years of bending over correspondence and the endless figures and calculations; old Fräulein Steinbeiss, who flitted about all day long with a cloth and a feather duster; and the two attendants, Hermann Müller and Heinrich Müller (no relation, as they incessantly insisted), who stood on either side of the monumental cash register, invariably wearing waistcoats and sleeve bands, and treated customers with the condescension that comes naturally, as it were, to those who occupy a higher station in life. Paul's father Theo Bereyter, though, whenever he, the emporium proprietor himself, came down to the shop for an hour or so (as he did every day) in his frock coat or a pin-striped suit and spats, would take up a position between the two potted palms, which would be either inside or outside the swing door depending on the weather, and would escort every single customer into the emporium with the most respectful courtesy, regardless of whether it was the neediest resident from the old people's home across the road or the opulent wife of Hastreiter, the brewery owner, and then see them out again with his compliments.

The emporium, Mme Landau added, being the only large store in the town and indeed in the entire district, by all accounts ensured a good middle class standard of living for the Bereyter family, and even one or two extravagances, as is evident (said Mme Landau) from the mere fact that Theodor drove a Dürkopp in the Twenties, attracting excited interest

as far afield as the Tyrol, Ulm or Lake Constance, as Paul liked to recall. Theodor Bereyter died on Palm Sunday, 1936; this too I heard from Mme Landau, who must have talked endlessly to Paul about these things, as I came to realize more clearly with every visit. The cause of death was given as heart failure, but in fact, as Mme Landau emphasized, he had died from the fury and fear that had been consuming him ever since, precisely two years before his death, the Jewish families, resident in his home town of Gunzenhausen for generations, had been the target of violent attacks. The emporium owner, escorted only by his wife and those in his employ, was buried before Easter in a remote corner, reserved for suicides and people of no denomination, behind a low wall in the churchyard at S. It is worth mentioning in this connection, said Mme Landau, that although the emporium, which passed to the widow, Thekla, could not be "Aryanized" after Theodor Bereyter's death, the family nonetheless had to sell it for next to nothing to Alfons Kienzle, a livestock and real estate agent who had recently set up as a respectable businessman. After this dubious transaction Thekla Bereyter fell into a depression and died within a few weeks.

All of these occurrences, Mme Landau said, Paul followed from afar without being able to intervene. On the one hand, when the bad news reached him it was always already too late to do anything, and, on the other, his powers of decision had been in some way impaired, making it impossible for him to think even as far as a single day ahead. For this reason, Mme Landau explained, Paul for a long time had only a partial grasp of what had happened in S in 1935 and 1936, and did not care to correct his patchy knowledge of the past. It was only in the last decade of his life, which he largely spent in Yverdon, that reconstructing those events became important to him, indeed vital, said Mme Landau. Although he was losing his sight, he spent many days in archives, making endless notes – on the events in Gunzenhausen, for instance, on that Palm Sunday of 1934, years before what became known as the Kristallnacht, when the windows of Jewish homes were smashed and the Jews themselves were hauled out of their hiding places in cellars and dragged through the streets. What horrified Paul was not only the coarse offences and the violence of those Palm Sunday incidents in Gunzenhausen, not only the death of seventy-five-year-old Ahron Rosenfeld, who was stabbed, or of thirty-year-old Siegfried Rosenau, who was hanged from a railing; it was not only these things, said Mme Landau, that horrified Paul, but also, nearly as deeply, a newspaper article he came across, reporting with *Schadenfreude* that the schoolchildren of Gunzenhausen had helped themselves to a free bazaar in the town the following morning, taking several weeks' supply of hair slides, chocolate cigarettes, coloured pencils, fizz powder and many other things from the wrecked shops.

What I was least able to understand in Paul's story, after all that, was the fact that in early 1939 – be it because the position of a German tutor in France in times that were growing more difficult was no longer tenable, or out of blind rage or even a sort of perversion – he went back to Germany, to the capital of the Reich, to Berlin, a city with which he was quite unfamiliar. There he took an office job at a garage in Oranienburg, and a few months later he was called up; those who were only three-quarter Aryans were apparently included in the muster. He served, if that is the word, for six years, in the motorized artillery, variously stationed in the Greater German homeland and in the several countries that were occupied. He was in Poland, Belgium, France, the Balkans, Russia and the Mediterranean, and doubtless saw more than

any heart or eye can bear. The seasons and the years came and went. A Walloon autumn was followed by an unending white winter near Berdichev, spring in the Departement Haute-Saône, summer on the coast of Dalmatia or in Romania, and always, as Paul wrote under this photograph,

one was, as the crow flies, about 2,000 km away – but from where? – and day by day, hour by hour, with every beat of the pulse, one lost more and more of one's qualities, became less comprehensible to oneself, increasingly abstract.

Paul's return to Germany in 1939 was an aberration, said Mme Landau, as was his return to S after the war, and to his teaching life in a place where he had been shown the door. Of course, she added, I understand why he was drawn back to school. He was quite simply born to teach children – a veritable Melammed, who could start from nothing and hold the most inspiring of lessons, as you yourself have described to me. And furthermore, as a good teacher he would have believed that one could consider those twelve wretched years over and done with, and simply turn the page and begin afresh. But that is no more than half the explanation, at most. What moved and perhaps even forced Paul to return, in 1939 and in 1945, was the fact that he was a German to the marrow, profoundly attached to his native land in the foothills of the Alps, and even to that miserable place S as well, which in fact he loathed and, deep within himself, of that I am quite sure, said Mme Landau, would have been pleased to see destroyed and obliterated, together with the townspeople, whom he found so utterly repugnant. Paul, said Mme Landau, could not abide the new flat that he was more or less forced to move into shortly before he retired, when the wonderful old Lerchenmüller house was pulled down to make way for a hideous block of flats; but even so, remarkably, in all of those last twelve years that he was living here in Yverdon he could never bring himself to give up that flat. Quite the contrary, in fact: he would make a special journey to S several times a year especially to see that all was in order, as he put it. Whenever he returned from one of those expeditions, which generally took just two days, he would always be in the gloomiest of spirits, and in his childishly appealing way he would rue the fact that, to his own detriment, he had once again ignored my urgent advice not to go there any more.

Here in Bonlieu, Mme Landau told me on another occasion, Paul spent a lot of time gardening, which I think he loved more than anything else. After we had left Salins and our decision had been taken that from now on he would live in Bonlieu, he asked me if he might take the garden in hand, which at that time was fairly neglected. And Paul really did transform the garden, in a quite spectacular manner. The young trees, the flowers, the plants and climbers, the shady ivy beds, the rhododendrons, the roses, the shrubs and perennials – they all grew, not a bare patch anywhere. Every afternoon, weather permitting, said Mme Landau, Paul was busy in the garden. But sometimes he would simply sit for a while, gazing at the greenery that burgeoned all around him. The doctor who had operated on his cataracts had advised him that peaceful spells spent simply looking at the leaves would protect and improve his eyesight. Not, of course, that Paul took any notice whatsoever of the doctor's orders at night, said Mme Landau. His light was always on till the small hours. He read and read – Altenberg, Trakl, Wittgenstein, Friedell, Hasenclever, Toller, Tucholsky, Klaus Mann, Ossietzky, Benjamin, Koestler and Zweig: almost all of them writers who had taken their own lives or had been close to doing so. He copied out passages into notebooks which give a good idea of how much the lives of these particular authors interested him. Paul copied out hundreds of pages, mostly in Gabelsberg shorthand because otherwise he would not have been able to write fast enough, and time and again one comes across stories of suicide. It seemed to me, said

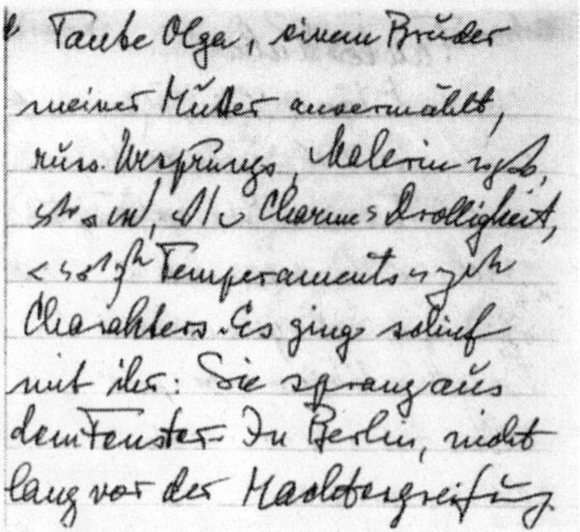
Taube Olga, einem Bruder
meiner Mutter anvermählt,
russ. Ursprungs, Malerin usw.,
[illegible] Charme, Drolligkeit,
[illegible] Temperaments u. [illegible]
Charakters. Es ging schief
mit ihr: Sie sprang aus
dem Fenster in Berlin, nicht
lang vor der Machtergreifung.

Mme Landau, handing me the black oilcloth books, as if Paul had been gathering evidence, the mounting weight of

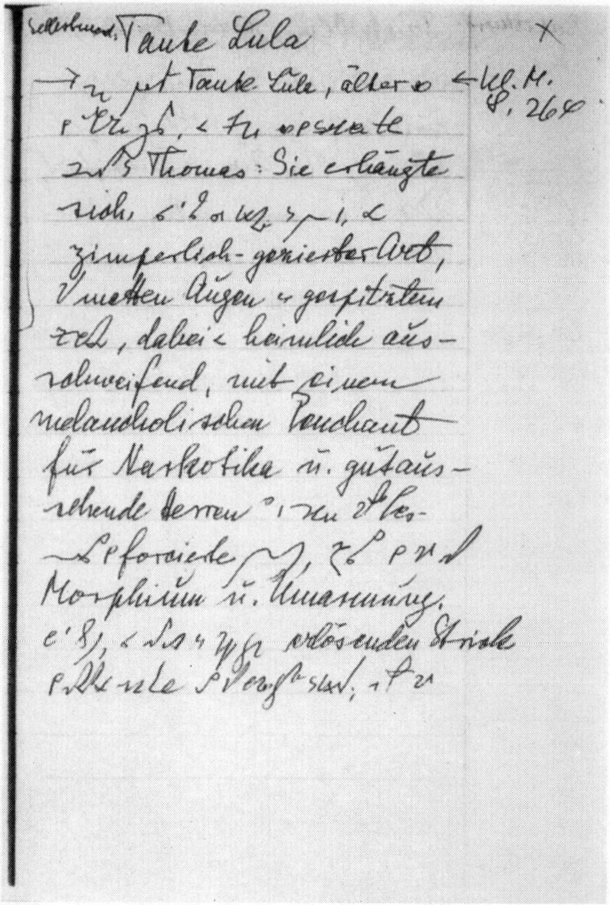

which, as his investigations proceeded, finally convinced him that he belonged to the exiles and not to the people of S.

In early 1982, the condition of Paul's eyes began to deteriorate. Soon all he could see were fragmented or shattered images. No second operation was going to be possible; Paul bore the fact with equanimity, said Mme Landau, and always looked back with immense gratitude to the eight years of light that the Berne operation had afforded him. If he paused to consider, Paul had said to her shortly after being given an extremely unfavourable prognosis, that as a child he had already been troubled with little dark patches and pearldrop shapes before his eyes, and had always been afraid that he would go blind at any time, then it was amazing, really, that his eyes had done him such good service for quite so long. The fact was, said Mme Landau, that Paul's whole manner at that time was extraordinarily composed as he contemplated the mouse-grey (his word) prospect before him. He realized then that the world he was about to enter might be a more confined one than that he had hitherto lived in, but he also believed there would be a certain sense of ease. I offered to read Paul the whole of Pestalozzi, said Mme Landau, to which he replied that for that he would gladly sacrifice his eyesight, and I should start right away, for preference, perhaps, with *The Evening Hour of a Hermit.* It was some time in the autumn, during one such reading hour, said Mme Landau, that Paul, without any preamble, informed me that there was now no reason to keep the flat in S and he proposed to give it up. Not long after Christmas we went to S to see to it. Since I had not set foot in the new Germany, I had misgivings as I looked forward to the journey. No snow had fallen, there was no sign anywhere of any winter tourism, and when we got out at S I felt as if we had arrived at the end of the world, and experienced so uncanny a premonition that I should have liked most of all to turn back on the spot. Paul's flat was cold and dusty and full of the past. For two or three days we busied ourselves in it aimlessly. On the third day a spell of mild *föhn* weather set in, quite unusual for the time of year. The pine forests were black on the mountainsides, the windows gleamed like lead, and the sky was so low and dark, one expected ink to run out of it any moment. The pain in my temples was so dreadful that I had to lie down, and I well remember that, when the aspirin Paul had given me gradually began to take effect, two strange, sinister patches began to move behind my eyelids, furtively. It was not till dusk that I woke; though on that day it was as early as three. Paul had covered me with a blanket, but he himself was nowhere to be seen. As I stood, irresolute in the hall, I noticed that Paul's windcheater was missing, which, as he had happened to mention that morning, had been hanging there for almost forty years. I knew at that moment that Paul had gone out, wearing that jacket, and that I would never see him alive again. So, in a way, I was ready when the doorbell rang soon after. It was only the manner in which he died, a death so inconceivable to me, that robbed me of my self-control at first; yet, as I soon realized, it was for Paul a perfectly logical step. Railways had always meant a great deal to him – perhaps he felt they were headed for death. Timetables and directories, all the logistics of railways, had at times become an obsession with him, as his flat in S showed. I can still see the Märklin model railway he had laid out on a deal table in the spare north-facing room: to me it is the very image and symbol of Paul's German tragedy. When Mme Landau said this, I thought of the stations, tracks, goods depots and signal boxes that Paul had so often drawn on the blackboard and which we had to copy into our exercise books as carefully as we could. It is hard, said Mme Landau, when I told her about those railway lessons, in the end it is hard to know what it is that

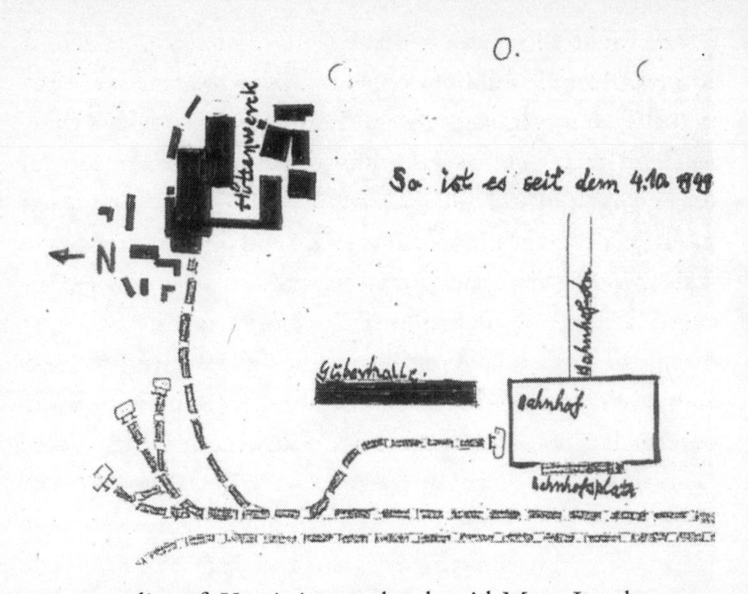

someone dies of. Yes, it is very hard, said Mme Landau, one really doesn't know. All those years that he was here in Yverdon I had no notion that Paul had found his fate already systematically laid out for him in the railways, as it were. Only once, obliquely, did he talk about his passion for railways, more as one talks of a quaint interest that belongs to the past. On that occasion, said Mme Landau, Paul told me that as a child he had once spent his summer holidays in Lindau, and had watched from the shore every day as the trains trundled across from the mainland to the island and from the island to the mainland. The white clouds of steam in the blue air, the passengers waving from the windows, the reflection in the water – this spectacle, repeated at intervals, so absorbed him that he never once appeared on time at the dinner table all that holiday, a lapse that his aunt responded to with a shake of the head that grew more resigned every time, and his uncle with the comment that he would end up on the railways.

When Paul told me this perfectly harmless holiday story, said Mme Landau, I could not possibly ascribe the importance to it that it now seems to have, though even then there was something about that last turn of phrase that made me uneasy. I suppose I did not immediately see the innocent meaning of Paul's uncle's expression, *end up on the railways*, and it struck me as darkly foreboding. The disquiet I experienced because of that momentary failure to see what was meant – I now sometimes feel that at that moment I beheld an image of death – lasted only a very short time, and passed over me like the shadow of a bird in flight.

AMBROS ADELWARTH

My field of corn is
but a crop of tears

I have barely any recollection of my own of Great-Uncle Adelwarth. As far as I can say with any certainty, I saw him only once, in the summer of 1951. That was when the Americans, Uncle Kasimir with Lina and Flossie, Aunt Fini with Theo and the little twins, and Aunt Theres, who was unmarried, came to stay with us in W for several weeks, either all together or one after the other. On one occasion during that time, the in-laws from Kempten and Lechbruck – emigrants, as is well known, tend to seek out their own kind – came to W for a few days, and it was at the resulting reunion of almost sixty members of the family that I saw my Great-Uncle Adelwarth, for the first (and, I believe, the last) time. Naturally, in the great upheaval caused by the visitors, in our own household and indeed throughout the whole village, since rooms had to be found elsewhere, he made no more impression on me at first than any of the others; but when he was called upon, as the eldest of the emigrants and their forefather, as it were, to address the gathered clan, that Sunday afternoon when we sat for coffee at the long trestle tables in the village hall, my attention was inevitably drawn to him as he rose and tapped his glass with a small spoon. Uncle Adelwarth was not particularly tall, but he was nonetheless a most distinguished presence who confirmed and enhanced the self-esteem of all who were there, as the general murmur of approval made clear – even though, as I, at the age of seven, immediately realized (in contrast to the adults, who were caught up in their own preconceptions), they seemed out-classed compared with this man. Although I do not remember what Uncle Adelwarth said in his rather formal address, I do recall being deeply impressed by the fact that his apparently effortless German was entirely free of any trace of our home dialect and that he used words and turns of phrase the meanings of which I could only guess at. After this, for me, truly memorable appearance, Uncle Adelwarth vanished from my sight for good when he left for Immenstadt on the mail bus the following day, and from there journeyed onward by rail to Switzerland. Not even in my thoughts did he remain present, and of his death two years later, let alone its circumstances, I knew nothing throughout my childhood, probably because the sudden end of Uncle Theo, who was felled by a stroke one morning while reading the paper, placed Aunt Fini and the twins in an extremely difficult situation, a turn of events which must have eclipsed the demise of an elderly relative who lived on his own. Moreover, Aunt Fini, whose closeness to him put her in the best position to tell us how things had been with Uncle Adelwarth, now found herself obliged (she wrote) to work night and day to see herself and the twins through, for which reason, understandably, she was the first to stop coming over from America for the summer months. Kasimir visited less and less often also, and only Aunt Theres came with any kind of regularity, for one thing because, being single, she was in by far the best position to do so, and for another because she was incurably homesick her whole life long. Three weeks after she arrived, on every visit, she would still be weeping with the joy of reunion, and three weeks before she left she would again be weeping with the pain of separation. If her stay with us was longer than six weeks, there would be a becalmed period in the middle that she would mostly fill with needlework; but if her stay was shorter there were times when one really did not know whether she was in tears because she was at home at long last or because she was already dreading having to leave again. Her last visit was a complete disaster. She wept in silence, at breakfast and at dinner, out walking in the fields or shopping for the Hummel figurines she doted on, doing crosswords or gazing out of the window. When we accompanied her to Munich, she sat streaming tears between us children in the back of Schreck the taxi driver's new Opel Kapitän as the roadside trees sped past us in the light of dawn, from Kempten to Kaufbeuren and from Kaufbeuren to Buchloe; and later I watched from the spectators' terrace as she walked towards the silvery aeroplane, with her hatboxes, across the tarmac at Riem airport, sobbing repeatedly and drying her eyes with a handkerchief. Without looking back once, she went up the steps and vanished through the dark opening into the belly of the aircraft – for ever, as one might say. For a while her weekly letters still reached us (invariably beginning: My dear ones at home, how are you? I am fine!) but then the correspondence, which had been kept up without fail for almost thirty years, broke off, as I noticed when the dollar bills that were regularly enclosed for me stopped coming. It was in the midst of carnival season that my mother put a death notice in the local paper, to the effect that our dear sister, sister-in-law and aunt had departed this life in New York following a short but bravely borne illness. All this prompted the talk again about Uncle Theo's far too early death, but not, as I well remember, of Uncle Adelwarth, who, like Theo, had died a few years or so before.

Our relatives' summer visits were probably the initial reason why I imagined, as I grew up, that I too would one day go to live in America. More important, though, to my dream of America was the different kind of everyday life displayed by the occupying forces stationed in our town. The local people found their moral conduct in general – to judge by comments sometimes whispered, sometimes spoken out loud – unbecoming in a victorious nation. They let the houses they had requisitioned go to ruin, put no window boxes on the balconies, and had wire-mesh fly screens in the windows instead of curtains. The womenfolk went about in trousers and dropped their lipstick-stained cigarette butts in the street, the men put their feet up on the table, the children left their bikes out in the garden overnight, and as for those negroes, no one knew what to make of them. It was precisely this kind of disparaging remark that strengthened my desire to see the one foreign country of which I had any idea at all. In the evenings, but particularly during the endless lessons at school, I pictured every detail of my future in America. This period of my imaginary Americanization, during which I crisscrossed the entire United States, now on horseback, now in a dark brown Oldsmobile, peaked between my sixteenth and seventeenth years in my attempt to perfect the mental and physical attitudes of a Hemingway hero, a venture in mimicry that was doomed to failure for various reasons that can easily be imagined. Subsequently my American dreams gradually faded away, and once they had reached vanishing point they were presently supplanted by an aversion to all things American. This aversion became so deeply rooted in me during my years as a student that soon nothing could have seemed more absurd to me than the idea that I might ever travel to America except under compulsion. Even so, I did eventually fly to Newark on the 2nd of January 1981. This change of heart was prompted by a photograph album of my mother's which had come into my hands a few months earlier and which contained pictures quite new to me of our relatives who had emigrated during the Weimar years. The longer I studied the photographs, the more urgently I sensed a growing need to learn more about the lives of the people in them. The photograph that follows here, for example, was taken in the Bronx

in March 1939. Lina is sitting on the far left, next to Kasimir. On the far right is Aunt Theres. I do not know who the other people on the sofa are, except for the little girl wearing glasses.

That's Flossie, who later became a secretary in Tucson, Arizona, and learnt to belly dance when she was in her fifties. The oil painting on the wall shows our village of W. As far as I have been able to discover, no one now knows the whereabouts of that picture. Not even Uncle Kasimir, who brought it with him to New York rolled up in a cardboard tube, as a farewell gift from his parents, knows where it can have got to.

So on that 2nd of January, a dark and dreary day, I drove south from Newark airport on the New Jersey turnpike in the direction of Lakehurst, where Aunt Fini and Uncle Kasimir, after they moved away from the Bronx and Mamaroneck in the mid Seventies, had each bought a bungalow in a so-called retirement community amidst the blueberry fields. Right outside the airport perimeter I came within an inch of driving off the road when a Jumbo rose ponderously into the air above a truly mountainous heap of garbage, like some creature from prehistoric times. It was trailing a greyish black veil of vapour, and for a moment it was as if it had spread its wings. Then I drove on into flat country, where for the entire length of the Garden State Parkway there was nothing but stunted trees, fields overgrown with heather, and deserted wooden houses, partly boarded up, with tumble-down cabins and chicken runs all around. There, Uncle Kasimir told me later, millions of hens were kept up to the postwar years, laying millions upon millions of eggs for the New York market till new methods of poultry-keeping made the business unprofitable and the smallholders and their birds disappeared. Shortly after nightfall, taking a side road that ran off from the Parkway for several kilometres through a kind of marshland, I reached the old peoples' town called Cedar Glen West. Despite the immense territory covered by this community, and despite the fact that the bungalow condominiums were indistinguishable from each other, and, furthermore, that almost identical glowing Father Christmases were standing in every front garden, I found Aunt Fini's house without difficulty, since everything at Cedar Glen West is laid out in a strictly geometrical pattern.

Aunt Fini had made *Maultaschen* for me. She sat at the table with me and urged me to help myself whilst she ate nothing, as old women often do when they cook for a younger relative who has come to visit. My aunt spoke about the past, sometimes covering the left side of her face, where she had had a bad neuralgia for weeks, with one hand. From time to time she would dry the tears that pain or her memories brought to her eyes. She told me of Theo's untimely death, and the years that followed, when she often had to work sixteen hours or more a day, and went on to tell me about Aunt Theres, and how, before she died, she had walked around for months as if she were a stranger to the place. At times, in the summer light, she had looked like a saint, in her white twill gloves which she had worn for years on account of her eczema. Perhaps, said Aunt Fini, Theres really was a saint. At all events she shouldered her share of troubles. Even as a schoolchild she was told by the catechist that she was a tearful sort, and come to think of it, said Aunt Fini, Theres really did seem to be crying most of her life. She had never known her without a wet handkerchief in her hand. And, of course, she was always giving everything away: all she earned, and whatever came her way as the keeper of the millionaire Wallerstein's household. As true as I'm sitting here, said Aunt Fini, Theres died a poor woman. Kasimir, and particularly Lina, doubted it, but the fact was that she left nothing but her collection of almost a hundred Hummel figurines, her wardrobe (which was splendid, mind you) and large quantities of paste jewellery – just enough, all told, to cover the cost of the funeral.

Theres, Kasimir and I, said Aunt Fini as we leafed through her photo album, emigrated from W at the end of

the Twenties. First, I took ship with Theres at Bremerhaven on the 6th of September 1927. Theres was twenty-three and I was twenty-one, and both of us were wearing bonnets. Kasimir followed from Hamburg in summer 1929, a few weeks before Black Friday. He had trained as a tinsmith, and was just as unable to find work as I was, as a teacher, or Theres, as a sempstress. I had graduated from the Institute at Wettenhausen the previous year, and from autumn 1926 I had worked as an unpaid teaching assistant at the primary school in W. This is a photograph taken at that time. We were on an outing to Falkenstein. The pupils all stood in the back of the

lorry, while I sat in the driver's cab with a teacher named Fuchsluger, who was one of the very first National Socialists, and Benedikt Tannheimer, who was the landlord of the Adler and the owner of the lorry. The child right at the back, with a cross marked over her head, is your mother,

Rosa. I remember, said Aunt Fini, that a month or so later, two days before I embarked, I went to Klosterwald with her, and saw her to her boarding school. At that time, I think, Rosa had a great deal of anxiety to contend with, given that her leaving home coincided so unhappily with her siblings' departure for another life overseas, for at Christmas she wrote a letter to us in New York in which she said she felt fearful when she lay awake in the dormitory at night. I tried to console her by saying she still had Kasimir, but then Kasimir left for America too, when Rosa was just fifteen. That's the way it always is, said Aunt Fini thoughtfully: one thing after another. Theres and I, at any rate, she continued after a while, had a comparatively easy time of it when we arrived in New York. Uncle Adelwarth, a brother of our mother, who had gone to America before the First World War and had been employed only in the best of houses since then, was able to find us positions immediately, thanks to his many connections. I became a governess with the Seligmans in Port Washington, and Theres a lady's maid to Mrs Wallerstein, who was about the same age and whose husband, who came from somewhere near Ulm, had made a considerable fortune with a number of brewing patents, a fortune that went on growing as the years went by.

Uncle Adelwarth, whom you probably do not remember any more, said Aunt Fini, as if a quite new and altogether more significant story were now beginning, was a man of rare distinction. He was born at Gopprechts near Kempten in 1886, the youngest of eight children, all of them girls except for him. His mother died, probably of exhaustion, when Uncle Adelwarth, who was given the name Ambros, was not yet two years old. After her death, the eldest daughter,

Kreszenz, who cannot have been more than seventeen at the time, had to run the household and play the role of mother as best she could, while their father the innkeeper sat with his customers, which was all he knew how to do. Like the other siblings, Ambros had to give Zenzi a hand quite early on, and at five he was already being sent to the weekly market at Immenstadt, together with Minnie, who was not much older, to sell the chanterelles and cranberries they had gathered the day before. Well into the autumn, said Aunt Fini, the two youngest of the Adelwarth children sometimes did nothing for weeks on end but bring home basketfuls of rosehips; they would cut them open, then dig out the hairy seeds with the tip of a spoon, and, after leaving them in a washtub for a few days to draw moisture, put the red flesh of the hips through the press. If one thinks now of the circumstances in which Ambros grew up, said Aunt Fini, one inevitably concludes that he never really had a childhood. When he was only thirteen he left home and went to Lindau, where he worked in the kitchens of the Bairischer Hof till he had enough for the rail fare to Lausanne, the beauties of which he had once heard enthusiastically praised at the inn in Gopprechts by a travelling watchmaker. Why, I shall never know, said Aunt Fini, but in my mind's eye I always see Ambros crossing Lake Constance from Lindau by steamer, in the moonlight, although that can scarcely have been how it was in reality. One thing is certain: that within a few days of leaving his homeland for good, Ambros, who was then fourteen at the outside, was working as an *apprenti garçon* in room service at the Grand Hôtel Eden in Montreux, probably thanks to his unusually appealing but nonetheless self-controlled nature. At least I think it was the Eden, said Aunt Fini, because, in one of the postcard albums that Uncle Adelwarth left, the world-famous hotel is on one of the opening pages, with its awnings lowered over the windows against the afternoon sun. During his apprenticeship in Montreux, Aunt Fini continued, after she had fetched the album from one of her bedroom drawers and opened it up before me, Ambros was

not only initiated into all the secrets of hotel life, but also learnt French to perfection, or rather, he absorbed it; he had the special gift of acquiring a foreign language, without apparent effort and without any teaching aids, within a year or two, solely by making certain adjustments (as he once explained to me) to his inner self. Along with very accomplished New York English he also spoke a most elegant French and an extremely dignified German, which astounded me the most, since he could hardly have had it from Gopprechts. Furthermore, Aunt Fini recalled, he had a far from elementary knowledge of Japanese, as I once discovered by chance when we were shopping together at Sacks' and he came to the rescue of a Japanese gentleman who knew no English and was embroiled in some unpleasantness.

Once his Swiss apprentice years were over, Ambros went to London, with excellent recommendations and testimonials, where he took a job at the Savoy Hotel in the Strand in the autumn of 1905, again in room service. It was in his London period that the mysterious episode of the lady from Shanghai occurred. All I know of her is that she had a taste for brown kid gloves; although Uncle Adelwarth did make occasional references later to what he had experienced with this lady (she marked the beginning of my career in misfortune, he once said), I never managed to find out the true facts of the matter. I assume that the lady from Shanghai – whom I always associated, doubtless absurdly, with Mata Hari – often stayed at the Savoy, and that Ambros, who was now about twenty, had contact with her professionally, if one can put it like that. It was the same with the counsellor from the Japanese legation whom he accompanied – in 1907, if I am not mistaken – on a journey by ship and rail via Copenhagen, Riga, St Petersburg, and Moscow, right across Siberia, to Japan, where the unmarried gentleman had a wonderful house set in a lake, near Kyoto. Ambros spent almost two years, partly as valet and partly as the counsellor's guest, in that floating and well-nigh empty house, and as far as I am aware he felt happier there than he had been anywhere else until then. Once, at Mamaroneck, said Aunt Fini, Uncle Adelwarth spent all of one afternoon telling me about his time in Japan. But I no longer remember exactly what he told me. Something about paper walls, I think, about archery, and a good deal about evergreen laurel, myrtle and wild camellia. And I remember something about

an old hollow camphor tree which supposedly had room for fifteen people inside it, a story of a decapitation, and the call of the Japanese cuckoo, said Aunt Fini, her eyes half closed, *hototogisu*, which he could imitate so well.

After morning coffee on the second day of my stay at Cedar Glen West, I went over to Uncle Kasimir. It was about half past ten when I sat down at the kitchen table with him. Lina was already busy at the stove. My uncle had produced two glasses and poured out the gentian brandy I had brought. In those days, he began, once I had managed to steer the talk to the subject of emigration, people like us simply had no chance in Germany. Only once, when I had finished my tinsmith apprenticeship in Altenstadt, did I get work, in '28, when they were putting a new copper roof on the synagogue in Augsburg. The Jews of Augsburg had donated the old copper roof for the war effort during the First World War,

and it wasn't till '28 that they had the money they needed for a new roof. This is me, said Uncle Kasimir, pushing across the table a framed postcard-size photograph he had taken down from the wall – at the far right, from where you're looking. But after that job there was nothing again for weeks, and one of my mates, Josef Wohlfahrt, who still felt confident about things when we were at work up on the synagogue roof, later hanged himself in despair. Fini wrote enthusiastic letters from her new homeland, so it was no wonder that I finally decided to follow my sisters to America. Of the rail journey across Germany I remember nothing, except that everything seemed unfamiliar and incomprehensible to me – the country we passed through, the huge railway stations and cities, the Rhineland and the vast flatlands up north – most probably because I had never been beyond the Allgäu and the Lechfeld region. But I do still see the offices of Norddeutscher Lloyd in Bremerhaven quite clearly in front of me. The passengers with little money were obliged to wait there till they could embark. I particularly remember the many different kinds of head-gear the emigrants wore: hoods and caps, winter and summer hats, shawls and kerchiefs, and then the peaked caps of the shipping line's stewards and the customs officers, and the bowler hats of the brokers and agents. On the walls hung large oil pictures of the ocean liners of the Lloyd fleet. Every one of them was cleaving a course full steam ahead, the bow rearing up out of the waves, conveying a sense of an unstoppable force driving onward. Above the door through which we finally left was a circular clock with Roman numerals, and over the clock, in ornate lettering, was the motto *Mein Feld ist die Welt.*

Aunt Lina was pushing boiled potatoes through a press onto a floured pastryboard, and Uncle Kasimir, pouring me another gentian, went on to describe his crossing in the teeth of the February storms. The way the waves rose up from the deep and came rolling on was terrifying, he said. Even as a child I used to be horrified when the frog pond was frozen over, and we played curling on the ice, and I would suddenly think of the darkness under my feet. And now, nothing but black water all around, day in, day out, and the ship always seeming to be in the selfsame place. Most of my fellow travellers were sea-sick. Exhausted they lay in their berths, their eyes glassy or half closed. Others squatted on the floor, stood leaning for hours against a wall, or tottered along the passageways like sleepwalkers. For a full week, I too felt like death. I did not begin to feel better until we cleared the Narrows into Upper Bay. I sat on a bench on deck. The ship had already slowed. I felt a light breeze on my forehead, and as we approached the waterfront Manhattan rose higher and higher before us out of the sunshot morning mists.

My sisters, who were waiting for me on the quayside,

were not able to be of much help, nor could Uncle Adelwarth find anything for me, because I was no use as a gardener or cook or servant. On the day after my arrival I rented a back room that looked out on a narrow air shaft, from Mrs Risa Litwak in Bayard Street on the Lower East Side. Mrs Litwak, whose husband had died the year before, spent the whole day cooking and cleaning, or if she wasn't cooking and cleaning she was making paper flowers or sewing all night for her children or for other people, or as a supply sempstress for some business or other. Sometimes she played on a pianola very pretty songs that I seemed to know from somewhere. Until the First World War, the Bowery and the whole Lower East Side were the districts where the immigrants chiefly came to live. More than a hundred thousand Jews arrived there every year, moving into the cramped, dingy apartments in the five- or six-storey tenement blocks. The so-called parlour, which faced the street, was the only room that had two windows, and the fire escape ran past one of them. In the autumn, the Jews would build their sukkahs on the fire escape landings, and in summer, when the heat hung motionless in the city streets for weeks and life was unbearable indoors, hundreds and thousands of people would sleep outside, up in the airy heights, or even on the roofs or sidewalks or the little fenced-off patches of grass on Delancey Street and in Seward Park. The whole of the Lower East Side was one huge dormitory. Even so, the immigrants were full of hope in those days, and I myself was by no means despondent when I started to look for a job at the end of February '28. And before the week was out I already had my place at a workbench, at the Seckler & Margarethen Soda and Seltzers Works near the sliproad up to Brooklyn Bridge. There I made stainless-steel boilers and vats of various sizes, and old Seckler, who was a Jew from Brünn (I never did find out who Margarethen was), sold most of them as "catering equipment" to illicit distilleries where the concern was far less about the asking price than about doing business with the utmost discretion. Seckler, who for some reason took a liking to me, said that the sale of these steel vats and all the rest of the plant

vital to the distilleries had developed as a side-line almost by itself, without his doing anything to encourage it, alongside the main business of the soda and seltzers works, and so he simply did not have the heart to cut it back. Seckler always praised my work, but he was reluctant to pay, and gave a poor wage. At least with me, he would say, you are on the first rung of the ladder. And then one day, it was a few weeks after Passover, he called me in to his office, leaned back in his chair, and said: Have you got a head for heights? If you have, you can go over to the new Yeshiva, they need metalworkers like you. And he gave me the address – 500 West 187th Street, corner Amsterdam Avenue. The very next day I was up on the top of the tower, just as I had been on the Augsburg Synagogue, only much higher, helping to rivet copper bands that were almost six metres wide onto the cupola that crowned the building, which looked like a cross between a railway station and an oriental palace. After that, I worked a lot on the tops of skyscrapers, which they went

on building until the early Thirties in New York, despite the Depression. I put the copper hoods on the General Electric Building, and from '29 to '30 we spent a year on the sheet-steel work on the summit of the Chrysler Building, which was unbelievably difficult on account of the curvatures and slopes. Since all my acrobatics were done two or three hundred metres above the ground, I naturally made a lot of money, but I spent it as fast as I earned it. And then I broke my wrist skating in Central Park and had no work till '34. And then we moved to the Bronx, and life up in the dizzy heights came to an end.

After lunch, Uncle Kasimir became visibly restless and paced to and fro, and at length he said: I have got to get out of the house! – to which Aunt Lina, who was washing up, replied: What a day to go for a drive! One might indeed have thought that night was falling, so low and inky black was the sky. The streets were deserted. We passed very few other cars on the road. It took us almost an hour to cover the thirty kilometres to the Atlantic, because Uncle Kasimir drove more slowly than I have ever known anyone drive on an open stretch of road. He sat angled up against the wheel, steering with his left hand and telling tales of the heyday of Prohibition. Occasionally he would take a glance ahead to check that we were still in the right lane. The Italians did most of the business, he said. All along the coast, in places like Leonardo, Atlantic Highlands, Little Silver, Ocean Grove, Neptune City, Belmar and Lake Como, they built summer palaces for their families and villas for their women and usually a church as well and a little house for a chaplain. Uncle slowed down even more and wound his window down. This is Toms River, he said, there's no one here in the winter. In the harbour, sailboats lay pushed up together like a frightened flock, rigging rattling. Two seagulls perched on top of a coffee shop built to look like a gingerbread house. The Buyright Store, the Pizza Parlour and the Hamburger Heaven were closed, and the private homes were locked up and shuttered too. The wind blew sand across the road and under the wooden sidewalks. The dunes, said Uncle, are invading the town. If people didn't keep coming in the summer, this would all be buried in a few years. From Toms River the road ran down to Barnegat Bay and across Pelican Island to the eighty-kilometre spit of land that stretches along the coast of New Jersey and is nowhere more than a kilometre or so wide. We parked the car and walked along the beach, with a biting northeasterly at our backs. I'm afraid I don't know much about Ambros Adelwarth, said Uncle Kasimir. When I arrived in New York he was already over forty, and in the early days, and later too, I hardly saw him more than once or twice a year. As far as his legendary past was concerned, of course there were rumours, but all I know for certain is that Ambros was major-domo and butler with the Solomons, who had an estate at Rocky Point, at the furthermost tip of Long Island, surrounded by water on

three sides. The Solomons – with the Seligmanns, the Loebs, the Kuhns, the Speyers and the Wormsers – were amongst the wealthiest of the Jewish banking families in New York. Before Ambros became the Solomons' butler he was valet and travelling companion to Cosmo, the Solomons' son, who was a few years younger than himself and was notorious in New York society for his extravagance and his eternal escapades. On one occasion, for instance, they said he had tried to ride a horse up the stairs in the lobby of The Breakers Hotel in Palm Beach. But I know stories like that only from hearsay. Fini, who became a sort of confidante for Ambros towards the end, sometimes hinted that there was something tragic about the relationship between Ambros and the Solomons' son. And, as far as I know, young Solomon really was destroyed by some mental illness in the mid Twenties. As for Uncle Adelwarth, all I can say is that I always felt sorry for him, because he could never, his whole life long, permit anything to ruffle his composure. Of course, said Uncle Kasimir, he was of the other persuasion, as anyone could see, even if the family always ignored or glossed over the fact. Perhaps some of them never realized. The older Uncle Adelwarth grew, the more hollowed-out he seemed to me, and the last time I saw him, in the house at Mamaroneck that the Solomons had left him, so finely furnished, it was as if his clothes were holding him together. As I said, Fini looked after him till the end. She'll be able to give you a better idea of what he was like. Uncle Kasimir stopped and stood gazing out at the ocean. This is the edge of the darkness, he said. And in truth it seemed as if the mainland were submerged behind us and as if there were nothing above the watery waste but this narrow strip of sand running up to the north and down towards the south.

I often come out here, said Uncle Kasimir, it makes me feel that I am a long way away, though I never quite know from where. Then he took a camera out of his large-check jacket and took this picture, a print of which he sent me two years later, probably when he had finally shot the whole film, together with his gold pocket watch.

Aunt Fini was sitting in her armchair in the dark living room when I went in to her that evening. Only the glow of the street lights was on her face. The aches have eased off, she said, the pain is almost over. At first I thought I was only imagining that it was getting better, so slow was the improvement. And once I was almost without pain, I thought: if you move now, it'll start again. So I just stayed sitting here. I've been sitting here all afternoon. I couldn't say whether I mightn't have nodded off now and then. I think I was lost in my thoughts most of the time. My aunt switched on the little reading lamp but kept her eyes closed. I went out into the kitchen and made her two soft-boiled eggs, toast, and peppermint tea. When I took the tray in to her I turned the conversation back to Uncle Adelwarth. About two years after he arrived in America, said Aunt Fini, dunking a soldier into one of the eggs, Ambros took a position with the Solomons on Long Island. What happened to the counsellor at the Japanese legation, I can't remember now. At all events, Uncle quickly made his way at the Solomons'. Within an amazingly short time, old Samuel Solomon, who was very impressed by the unfailing sureness of Ambros in all things, offered him the position of personal attendant to his son, to watch over him, since he believed, not without reason, that great dangers lay in his path. There is no doubt that Cosmo Solomon, whom I never had the opportunity to meet, was inclined to eccentricity. He was extremely gifted, and a very promising student of engineering, but gave up his studies to build flying machines in an old factory in Hackensack. At the same time, mind you, he spent a lot of time at places like Saratoga Springs and Palm Beach, for one thing because he was an excellent polo player, for another because he could blow huge sums of money at luxury hotels like the Breakers, the Poinciana or the American Adelphi, which at that time, so Uncle Adelwarth once told me, was plainly the main thing as far as he was concerned. Old Solomon was worried by the dissipated life his son was leading, and felt it had no future. When he tried to cut back his allowance, which in point of fact had been unlimited, Cosmo hit upon the idea of opening up a source of income that would never dry up, by playing the casinos of Europe during the summer months. In June 1911, with Ambros as his friend and guide, he went to France for the first time, and promptly won considerable sums at Evian on Lake Geneva and then at Monte Carlo, in the Salle

Schmidt. Uncle Adelwarth once told me that Cosmo would become strangely detached when he was playing roulette. At first, Ambros would think he was concentrating on calculations of probability, till one day Cosmo told him that at such times he actually was in a trance of some kind, trying to decipher the right number as it appeared for a fraction of a second from out of mists that were ordinarily impenetrable, whereupon, without the slightest hesitation, and as it were still in a dream, he would place his bet, either *en plein* or *à cheval.* Cosmo claimed that this condition of total withdrawal from normal life was dangerous, and it was the task of Ambros to watch over him as one would over a sleeping child. Of course I do not know what was really going on, said Aunt Fini, but one thing is certain: at Evian and Monte Carlo, the two of them made such a killing that Cosmo was able to buy an aeroplane from Deutsch de la Meurthe, the French industrialist. He flew it in the Quinzaine d'Aviation de la Baie de Seine at Deauville that August, and was by far the most daring of them all at looping the loop. Cosmo was in Deauville with Ambros in the summer of 1912 and 1913 also, and caught the imagination of society, not just with his astounding luck at roulette and his daredevil acrobatics on the polo field but chiefly, I'm certain, by the fact that he turned down every invitation he received to tea, dinner or such like, and never went out or ate with anyone but Ambros, whom he always treated as an equal. Incidentally, said Aunt Fini, in Uncle Adelwarth's postcard album there is a picture that shows Cosmo with a trophy presented by an aristocratic lady – the Comtesse de FitzJames, if I remember rightly – after a match at the Clairefontaine Hippodrome, probably a charity event. It is the only photograph of Cosmo Solomon

that I possess. There are relatively few photos of Ambros, too, probably because, like Cosmo, he was very shy, despite his familiarity with the ways of the world. In the summer of 1913,

Aunt Fini continued, a new casino was opened at Deauville, and during the first few weeks people were seized by so frenetic a gambling fever that all the roulette and baccarat tables, and what they call the *petits chevaux*, were constantly occupied by players, and besieged by more who wanted to play. One well-known *joueuse* called Marthe Hanau supposedly masterminded the hysteria. I remember clearly, said Aunt Fini, that Uncle Adelwarth once called her a notorious *filibustière*, who had been a thorn in the flesh of the casino management for years but was now coaxing the gamblers to the tables on their behalf and at their behest. Apart from the machinations of Marthe Hanau, it was the overexcited atmosphere, which had been quite changed by the ostentatious luxury of the new casino, that was responsible for the unparalleled rise in the earnings of the Deauville Bank that summer of 1913, in Uncle Adelwarth's view. As for Cosmo, in the summer of 1913 he held even more aloof than in previous years from a social whirl that was growing ever headier, and would play only late in the evening, in the inner sanctum, the Salle de la Cuvette. Only gentlemen in dinner jackets were admitted to the *privé*, where the atmosphere that prevailed was always, as Uncle Adelwarth put it, most ominous – small wonder, said Aunt Fini, if you consider that whole fortunes, family properties, real estate and the achievements of lifetimes were not infrequently gambled away within hours. At the start of the season, Cosmo's luck was often changeable, but towards the end it would surpass even his own expectations. Eyes half closed, he would win time after time, pausing only when Ambros brought him a *consommé* or *café au lait*. Two evenings in a row, so Uncle Adelwarth told me, Cosmo cleaned out the bank and runners had to fetch more money, said Aunt Fini; and then on the third evening, when he broke the bank again, Cosmo won so much that Ambros was busy till dawn counting the money and packing it into a steamer trunk. After spending the summer in Deauville, Cosmo and Ambros travelled via Paris and Venice to Constantinople and Jerusalem. I cannot tell you anything of what happened on that journey, said Aunt Fini, because Uncle Adelwarth would never answer questions about it. But there is a photo of him in Arab

costume, taken when they were in Jerusalem, and, said Aunt Fini, I have a kind of diary too, in tiny writing, that Ambros kept. For a long time I had quite forgotten about it, but, strange to say, I tried only recently to decipher it. With my poor eyes, though, I could not make out much more of it than the odd word; perhaps you should give it a try.

With long pauses, during which she often seemed very far away and lost, Aunt Fini told me, on my last day at Cedar Glen West, of the end of Cosmo Solomon and the later years of my Great-Uncle Ambros Adelwarth. Shortly after the two globetrotters returned from the Holy Land, as Aunt Fini put it, the war broke out in Europe. The more it raged, and the more we learnt of the extent of the devastation, the less Cosmo was able to regain a footing in the unchanged daily life of America. He became a stranger to his former friends, he abandoned his apartment in New York City, and even out on Long Island he soon withdrew entirely to his own quarters and at length to a secluded garden house known as the summer villa. Aunt Fini said that one of the Solomons' old gardeners once told her that in those days Cosmo would often be steeped in melancholy all day, and then at night would pace to and fro in the unheated summer villa, groaning softly. Wildly agitated, he would string out words that bore some relation to the fighting, and as he uttered these words of war he would apparently beat his forehead with his hand, as if he were vexed at his own incomprehension or were trying to learn what he said by heart. Frequently he would be so beside himself that he no longer even recognized Ambros. And yet he claimed that he could see clearly, in his own head, what was happening in Europe: the inferno, the dying, the rotting bodies lying in the sun in open fields. Once he even took to cudgelling the rats he saw running through the trenches. When the war ended, Cosmo's condition temporarily improved. He went back to designing flying machines, drew up a scheme for a tower house on the coast of Maine, took to playing the cello again, studied maps and ocean charts, and discussed with Ambros the various travels he planned. To the best of my knowledge, they made only one of these journeys, in the early summer of 1923, when the two of them went to Heliopolis. One or two pictures have survived from that visit to Egypt: one shows a *kafeneion* in Alexandria called the Paradeissos, one the San Stefano casino at Ramleh, and one the casino at Heliopolis. Their visit to Egypt seems to have

been made at rather short notice, said Aunt Fini, and from what Uncle Adelwarth told me it was an attempt to regain the past, an attempt that appears to have failed in every respect. The start of Cosmo's second serious nervous breakdown appears to have been connected with a German film about a gambler that was screened in New York at the time, which Cosmo described as a labyrinth devised to imprison him and drive him mad, with all its mirror reversals. He was particularly disturbed by an episode towards the end of the film in which a one-armed showman and hypnotist by the name of Sandor Weltmann induced a sort of collective hallucination in his audience. From the depths of the stage (as Cosmo repeatedly described it to Ambros) the mirage image of an oasis appeared. A caravan emerged onto the stage from a grove of palms, crossed the stage, went down into the auditorium, passed amongst the spectators, who were craning round in amazement, and vanished as mysteriously as it had appeared. The terrible thing was (Cosmo insisted) that he himself had somehow gone from the hall together with the caravan, and now could no longer tell where he was. One day, not long after, Aunt Fini continued, Cosmo really did disappear. I do not know where they searched for him, or for how long, but know that Ambros finally found him two or three days later on the top floor of the house, in one of the nursery rooms that had been locked for years. He was standing on a stool, his arms hanging down motionless, staring out at the sea where every now and then, very slowly, steamers passed by, bound for Boston or Halifax. When Ambros asked why he had gone up there, Cosmo said he had wanted to see how his brother was. But he never did have a brother, according to Uncle Adelwarth. Soon after, when Cosmo's condition had improved to some extent, Ambros accompanied him to Banff in the Canadian Rockies, for

the good air, on the advice of the doctors. They spent the whole summer at the famous Banff Springs Hotel. Cosmo was then like a well-behaved child with no interest in anything and Ambros was fully occupied by his work and his increasing concern for his charge. In mid October the snows began. Cosmo spent many an hour looking out of the tower window at the vast pine forests all around and the snow swirling down from the impenetrable heights. He would hold his rolled-up handkerchief clenched in his fist and bite into it repeatedly out of desperation. When darkness fell he would lie down on the floor, draw his legs up to his chest and hide his face in his hands. It was in that state that Ambros had to take him home and, a week later, deliver him to the Samaria Sanatorium at Ithaca, New York, where that same year, without saying a word or moving a muscle, he faded away.

These things happened more than half a century ago, said Aunt Fini. At that time I was at the Institute in Wettenhausen and knew nothing of Cosmo Solomon, nor of our mother's brother who had emigrated from Gopprechts. It was a long time before I learnt anything of Uncle Adelwarth's earlier days, even after I arrived in New York, and despite the fact that I was always in touch with him. After Cosmo's death, he became butler in the house at Rocky Point. From 1930 to 1950 I regularly drove out to Long Island, either alone or with Theo, as an extra help when big occasions were being prepared, or simply to visit. In those days, Uncle Adelwarth had more than half a dozen servants under him, not counting the gardeners and chauffeurs. His work took all his time and energy. Looking back, you might say that Ambros Adelwarth the private man had ceased to exist, that nothing was left but his shell of decorum. I could not possibly have imagined him in his shirtsleeves, or in stockinged feet without his half-boots, which were unfailingly polished till they shone, and it was always a mystery to me when, or if, he ever slept, or simply rested a little. At that time he had no interest in talking about the past at all. All that mattered to him was that the hours and days in the Solomons' household should pass without any disruption, and that the interests and ways of old Solomon should not conflict with those of the second Mrs Solomon. From about the time he was thirty-five, said Aunt Fini, this became particularly difficult for Uncle Adelwarth, given that old Solomon had announced one day, without preamble, that he would no longer be present at any dinners or gatherings whatsoever, that he would no longer have anything at all to do with the outside world, and that he was going to devote himself entirely to growing orchids, whereas the second Mrs Solomon, who was a good twenty years younger than him, was known far beyond New York for her weekend parties, for which guests generally arrived on Friday afternoons. So on the one hand Uncle Adelwarth was increasingly kept busy looking after old Solomon, who practically lived in his hothouses, and on the other he was fully occupied in pre-empting the second Mrs Solomon's characteristic liking for tasteless indiscretions. Presumably the demands made by these twofold duties wore him down more, in the long term, than he admitted to himself, especially during the war years, when old Solomon, scandalized by the stories that still reached him in his seclusion, took to spending most of his time sitting wrapped in a travelling rug in an overheated glasshouse amidst the pendulous air-roots of his South American plants, uttering scarcely a syllable beyond the bare essentials, while Margo Solomon persisted in holding court. But when old Solomon died in his wheelchair in the early months of 1947, said Aunt Fini, something curious happened: now it was Margo who, having ignored her husband for nearly ten years, could hardly be persuaded to leave her room. Almost all the staff were discharged. Uncle Adelwarth's principal duty was now to look after the house, which was well-nigh deserted and largely draped with white dust-sheets. That was when Uncle Adelwarth began, now and again, to recount to me incidents from his past life. Even the least of his reminiscences, which he fetched up very slowly from depths that were evidently unfathomable, was of astounding precision, so that, listening to him, I gradually became convinced that Uncle Adelwarth had an infallible memory, but that, at the same time, he scarcely allowed himself access to it. For that reason, telling stories was as much a torment to him as an attempt at self-liberation. He was at once saving himself, in some way, and mercilessly destroying himself. As if to distract me from her last words, Aunt Fini picked up one of the albums from the side table. This, she said, opening it and passing it over to me, is Uncle

Adelwarth as he was then. As you can see, I am on the left with Theo, and on the right, sitting beside Uncle, is his sister Balbina, who was just then visiting America for the first time. That was in May 1950. A few months after the picture was taken, Margo Solomon died of the complications of Banti's disease. Rocky Point passed to various beneficiaries and was sold off, together with all the furniture and effects, at an auction that lasted several days. Uncle Adelwarth was sorely affected by the dispersal, and a few weeks later he moved into the house at Mamaroneck that old Solomon had made over to him before he died. There is a picture of the living room on one of the next pages, said Aunt Fini. The whole house was always very neat and tidy, down to the last detail, like the room in this photograph. Often it seemed to me as if Uncle

Adelwarth was expecting a stranger to call at any moment. But no one ever did. Who would, said Aunt Fini. So I went over to Mamaroneck at least twice a week. Usually I sat in the blue armchair when I visited, and Uncle sat at his bureau, at a slight angle, as if he were about to write something or other. And from there he would tell me stories and many a strange tale. At times I thought the things he said he had witnessed, such as beheadings in Japan, were so improbable that I supposed he was suffering from Korsakov's syndrome: as you may know, said Aunt Fini, it is an illness which causes lost memories to be replaced by fantastic inventions. At any rate, the more Uncle Adelwarth told his stories, the more desolate he became. After Christmas '52 he fell into such a deep depression that, although he plainly felt a great need to talk about his life, he could no longer shape a single sentence, nor utter a single word, or any sound at all. He would sit at his bureau, turned a little to one side, one hand on the desktop pad, the other in his lap, staring steadily at the floor. If I talked to him about family matters, about Theo or the twins or the new Oldsmobile with the white-walled tyres, I could never tell if he were listening or not. If I tried to coax him out into the garden, he wouldn't react, and he refused to consult a doctor, too. One morning when I went out to Mamaroneck, Uncle Adelwarth was gone. In the mirror of the hall stand he had stuck a visiting card with a message for me, and I have carried it with me ever since. Have gone to Ithaca. Yours

Have gone to Ithaca.

Ambrose Adelwarth
123 Lebanon Drive
Mamaroneck
New York

Yours ever – Ambrose.

ever – Ambrose. It was a while before I understood what he meant by Ithaca. Needless to say, I drove over to Ithaca as often as I could in the weeks and months that followed. Ithaca is in a beautiful part of the country. All around there are forests and gorges through which the water rushes down towards the lake. The sanatorium, which was run by a Professor Fahnstock, was in grounds that looked like a park. I still remember, said Aunt Fini, standing with Uncle Adelwarth by his window one crystal-clear Indian Summer morning. The air was coming in from outside and we were looking over the almost motionless trees towards a meadow that reminded me of the Altach marsh when a middle-aged man appeared, holding a white net on a pole in front of him and occasionally taking curious jumps. Uncle Adelwarth stared straight ahead, but he registered my bewilderment all the same, and said: It's the butterfly man, you know. He comes round here quite often. I thought I caught an undertone of mockery in the words, and so took them as a sign of the improvement that Professor Fahnstock felt had been effected by the electroconvulsive therapy. Later in the autumn, though, the extent of the harm that had been done to Uncle's spirit and body was becoming clearer. He grew thinner and thinner, his hands, which used to be so calm, trembled, his face became lopsided, and his left eye moved restlessly. The last time I visited Uncle Adelwarth was in November. When it was time for me to leave, he insisted on seeing me to my car. And for that purpose he specially put on his *paletot* with the black velvet collar, and his Homburg. I still see him standing there in the driveway, said Aunt Fini, in that heavy overcoat, looking very frail and unsteady.

The morning I left Cedar Glen West was icy and dark. Exactly as she had described Uncle Adelwarth the day before, Aunt Fini now stood on the pavement in front of her bungalow, in a dark winter coat that was too heavy for her, waving a handkerchief after me. As I drove off I could see her in the mirror, with clouds of white exhaust about her, growing smaller and smaller; and, as I recall that mirror image, I find myself thinking how strange it is that no one since then has waved a handkerchief after me in farewell. In the few days I still had in New York I began making my notes on the inconsolable Aunt Theres, and about Uncle Kasimir on the roof of the Augsburg Synagogue. But my thoughts kept returning to Ambros Adelwarth in particular, and whether I ought not to see the sanatorium at Ithaca which he had entered voluntarily in his sixty-seventh year and where he had subsequently perished. At the time, true, the idea remained a mere thought, either because I did not want to waste my air ticket back to London or because I was wary of looking more closely into the matter. It was not until the early summer of 1984 that I finally went to Ithaca, having meanwhile taken great pains to decipher Uncle Adelwarth's travel notes of 1913 and having concluded that, if I intended to go to Ithaca, I ought not to defer it any longer. So I flew once more to New York and drove northwest along Highway 17 the same day, in a hired car, past various sprawling townships which, though some of their names were familiar, all seemed to be in the middle of nowhere. Monroe, Monticello, Middletown, Wurtsboro, Wawarsing, Colchester and Cadosia, Deposit, Delhi, Neversink and Niniveh – I felt as if I and the car I sat in were being guided by remote control through an outsize toyland where the place names had been picked at random by some invisible giant child, from the ruins of another world long since abandoned. It was as if the car had a will of its own on the broad highway. As all vehicles moved at almost the same speed, overtaking, when it occurred at all, went so slowly that I began to feel like a travelling companion of my neighbour in the next lane as I inched my way forward. At one point, for instance, I drove in the company of a black family for a good half hour. They waved and smiled repeatedly to show that I already had a place in their hearts, as a friend of the family, as it were, and when they parted from me in a broad curve at the Hurleyville exit – the children pulling clownish faces out of the rear window – I felt deserted and desolate for a time. The countryside began to look more uninhabited too. The road crossed a great plateau, with hills and undulations to the right, rising to mountains of some height towards the northerly horizon. Just as the winter days I had spent in America three years before had been dark and colourless, so now the earth's surface, a patchwork of greens, was flooded with light. In the long since abandoned pastures stretching towards the mountains grew clumps of oaks and alders; rectilinear plantations of spruces alternated with irregular stands of birches and aspens, the countless trembling leaves of which had opened only a week or so before; and even on the dark, distant slopes, where pine forests covered the mountainsides, the pale green of larches lit by the evening sun gleamed here and there in the background. When I saw those seemingly uninhabited highlands, I remembered the longing for faraway places that I had known when I bent over my atlas as a pupil at the monastery school, and how often I had travelled, in my thoughts, across the states of America, which I could recite by heart in alphabetical order. In the course of a geography lesson that lasted very nearly an eternity – outside, the early morning blue was still untouched by noonday brightness – I had once explored the regions I was now driving through, as well as the Adirondacks further to the north, which Uncle Kasimir had told me looked just like home. I still remember searching the map with a magnifying glass for the source of the Hudson River, and getting lost in a map square with a great many mountains and lakes. Certain place names such as Sabattis, Gabriels, Hawkeye, Amber Lake, Lake Lila and Lake Tear-in-the-Clouds have remained indelibly in my memory ever since.

At Owego, where I had to turn off the State Highway, I took a break and sat till almost nine in a roadside café, occasionally jotting down a word or two but mostly staring out absent-mindedly through the panoramic windows at the endless traffic and the western sky, still streaked with orange, flamingo pink and gold long after the sun had set. And so it was already late in the evening when I arrived in Ithaca. For maybe half an hour I drove around the town and its suburbs, to get my bearings, before pulling up at a guesthouse in a side street, silent and lit up in its dark garden, like the "Empire des Lumières" in which no one has ever set foot. A path curved from the pavement and ended in a flight of stone steps at the front door, where a shrub stretched out horizontal branches bearing white blossom. In the lamplight I thought for a moment that they were covered with snow. Everyone was plainly already asleep, and it was some time before an aged porter emerged from the depths of the house. He was so doubled over that he cannot have been able to see more than the lower half of anyone standing in front of him. Because of this handicap, no doubt, he had already taken a quick glance at the latecomer outside the glazed door before he crossed the hall, a glance that was the more penetrating for being brief. Without a word he escorted me up a fine mahogany staircase to the top floor, where he showed me to a spacious room overlooking the back garden. I put down my bag, opened one of the high windows, and looked out into the heaving shadows of a cypress that soared up from the depths. The air was filled with its scent and with an unceasing rushing sound, made not by the wind in the trees, as I supposed at first, but by the

Ithaca Falls, which were a short distance away, though invisible from my window. Before I arrived in the town it had been impossible to imagine that in the Lake Cayuga region more than a hundred such falls have been tumbling into the deep-carved gorges and valleys ever since the Ice Age. I lay down and immediately fell into a deep sleep, exhausted by the long journey. The powdery veils that rose silently from the roar of the Falls drifted into my sleep like white curtains blown into a room black with night. The next morning I searched the telephone books in vain for the Samaria Sanatorium or the Professor Fahnstock mentioned by Aunt Fini. Nor was I any more successful when I called on a psychiatric practice, and when I asked the blue-rinsed lady at reception she visibly paled with horror at the words *private mental home.* As I was leaving the hotel to make enquiries in town, I met the crooked porter in the front garden, coming up the path with a broom. He listened to my request for information most attentively and then, leaning on his broom, thought in silence for a good minute. Fahnstock, he exclaimed at length, so loudly that he might have been talking to a deaf person, Fahnstock died in the Fifties. Of a stroke, if I am not mistaken. And in a few words that came with a rattle from his constricted chest he went on to tell me that Fahnstock had had a successor, one Dr Abramsky, though Abramsky had not taken any more patients into the sanatorium since the late Sixties. What he did nowadays in that old place on his own, said the porter, turning abruptly to go, no one knew. And from the door he called after me: I have heard say he's become a beekeeper.

The old porter's information enabled me to find the sanatorium without difficulty that afternoon. A long drive swept through a park that must have covered almost a hundred acres and led up to a villa built entirely of wood. With its covered verandahs and balconies it resembled a Russian dacha, or one of those immense pinewood lodges stuffed with trophies that Austrian archdukes and princes built all over their hunting grounds in Styria and the Tyrol in the late nineteenth century, to accommodate their aristocratic guests and the accredited barons of industry. So clear were the signs of decay, so singularly did the window panes flash in the sunlight, that I did not dare go any closer, and instead began by looking around the park, where conifers of almost every kind – Lebanese cedars, mountain hemlocks, Douglas firs, larches, Arolla and Monterey pines, and feathery swamp cypresses – had all grown to their full size. Some of the cedars and larches were forty metres tall, and one of the hemlocks must have been fifty. There were woodland meadows between the trees where bluebells, white cardamines and yellow goatsbeard grew side by side. In other parts of the park there were many different ferns, and the new greenery of dwarf Japanese maples, lit up by rays of sunlight, swayed over the fallen leaves underfoot. I had been strolling around the arboretum for almost an hour when I came upon Dr Abramsky busy fitting out new beehives outside his apiary. He was a stocky man close to sixty, and wore threadbare trousers. From the right pocket of his patched-up jacket protruded a goose wing, such as might once have been used as a hand brush. What struck one immediately about Dr Abramsky was his shock of thick, flaming red hair that stood on end as if he were in a state of the greatest anxiety; it reminded me of the Pentecostal tongues of fire over the heads of the disciples, depicted in my first catechism. Quite unperturbed by my appearance out of nowhere, Dr Abramsky pulled up a wicker chair for me and, going on with his work on the beehives, listened to my story. When I had finished he put his tools aside and began to talk himself. I never knew Cosmo Solomon, he said, but I did know your great-uncle, since I started here in 1949 at the age of thirty-one, as Fahnstock's assistant. I remember the Adelwarth case so clearly for a special reason. He came at the beginning of a complete change in my thinking, one that led me, in the decade following Fahnstock's death, to cut back my psychiatric practice more and more, and eventually to give it up altogether. Since mid May 1969 – I shall soon have been retired for fifteen years – I have spent my life out of doors here, in the boathouse or the apiary, depending on the weather, and I no longer concern myself with what goes on in the so-called real world. No doubt I am now, in some sense, mad; but, as you may know, these things are merely a question of perspective. You will have seen that the Samaria is now deserted. Giving it up was the step I had to take in order to free myself from any involvement in life. I do not expect anyone can really imagine the pain and wretchedness once stored up in this extravagant timber palace, and I hope all this misfortune will gradually melt away now as it falls apart. For a while Dr Abramsky said nothing, and merely gazed out into the distance. It is true, he said at length, that Ambrose Adelwarth was not committed into our care by any relative, but came to us of his own free will. Why he came here remained a mystery to me for a long time, and he never talked about it. Fahnstock diagnosed profound senile depression with a tendency to cataleptic seizures, though this was contradicted by the fact that Ambrose showed no sign at all of neglecting his person, as patients in that condition usually do. Quite the contrary, he attached the greatest importance to his appearance. I only ever saw him in a three-piece suit and wearing a flawlessly knotted bow tie. Nonetheless, even when he was simply standing at the window looking out he always gave the impression of being filled with some appalling grief. I do not think, said Dr Abramsky, that I have ever met a more melancholy person than your great-uncle; every casual utterance, every gesture, his entire deportment (he held himself erect until the end), was tantamount to a constant pleading for leave of absence. At meals – to which he always came, since he remained absolute in matters of courtesy even in his darkest times – he still helped himself, but what he actually ate was no more than the symbolic offerings that were once placed on the graves of the dead. It was also remarkable how readily Ambrose submitted to shock treatment, which in the early Fifties, as I understood only later, really came close to torture or martyrdom. Other patients often had to be frogmarched to the treatment room, said Dr Abramsky, but Ambrose would always be sitting on the stool outside the door at the appointed hour, leaning his head against the wall, eyes closed, waiting for what was in store for him.

In response to my request, Dr Abramsky described shock treatment in greater detail. At the start of my career in psychiatry, he said, I was of the opinion that electrotherapy was a humane and effective form of treatment. As students we had been taught – and Fahnstock, in his stories about clinical practice, had repeatedly described in graphic terms – how in the old days, when pseudo-epileptic fits were induced by injecting insulin, patients would be convulsed for minutes, seemingly on the point of death, their faces contorted and blue. Compared with this approach, the introduction of electric shock treatment, which could be dispensed with greater precision and stopped immediately if the patient's reaction was extreme, constituted a considerable step forward. In our view, it seemed completely legitimate once sedatives and muscle relaxants began to be used in the early Fifties, to avoid the worst of the incidental injuries, such as dislocated shoulders or jaws, broken teeth, or other fractures. Given these broad improvements in shock therapy, Fahnstock, dismissing my (alas) none too forceful objections with his characteristic lordliness, adopted what was known as the block method, a course of treatment advocated by the German psychiatrist Braunmühl, which not infrequently involved more than a hundred electric shocks at intervals of only a very few days. This would have been about six months before Ambrose joined us. Needless to say, when treatment was so frequent, there could be no question of proper documentation or assessment of the therapy; and that was what happened with your great-uncle too. Besides, said Dr Abramsky, all of the material on file – the case histories and the medical records Fahnstock kept on a daily basis, albeit in a distinctly cursory fashion – have probably long since been eaten by the mice. They took over the madhouse when it was closed and have been multiplying without cease ever since; at all events, on nights when there is no wind blowing I can hear a constant scurrying and rustling in the dried-out shell of the building, and at times, when a full moon rises beyond the trees, I imagine I can hear the pathetic song of a thousand tiny upraised throats. Nowadays I place all my hope in the mice, and in the woodworm and deathwatch beetles. The sanatorium is creaking, and in places already caving in, and sooner or later they will bring about its collapse. I have a recurring dream of that collapse, said Dr Abramsky, gazing at the palm of his left hand as he spoke. I see the sanatorium on its lofty rise, see everything simultaneously, the building as a whole and also the minutest detail; and I know that the woodwork, the roof beams, door posts and panelling, the floorboards and staircases, the rails and banisters, the lintels and ledges, have already been hollowed out under the surface, and that at any moment, as soon as the chosen one amongst the blind armies of beetles dispatches the very last, scarcely material resistance with its jaws, the entire lot will come down. And that is precisely what does happen in my dream, before my very eyes, infinitely slowly, and a great yellowish cloud billows out and disperses, and where the sanatorium once stood there is merely a heap of powder-fine wood dust, like pollen. Dr Abramsky's voice had grown softer as he spoke, but now, pausing first to review (as I supposed) the imaginary spectacle once more before his mind's eye, he returned to reality. Fahnstock, he resumed, had been trained in neurology at an asylum in Lemberg, immediately before the First World War: at a time, that is, when psychiatry was primarily concerned with subduing those in its custody, and keeping them in safe detention. For that reason he was naturally inclined to interpret the recurrent desolation and apathy of sick patients exposed to continued shock therapy, their growing inability to concentrate, their sluggishness of mind, their muted voices, and even cases when patients entirely ceased to speak, as signs of successful therapy. So to his mind the docility of Ambrose was a result of the new treatment. Ambrose was one of the first of our patients to undergo a series of shocks, over a period of weeks and months; but that docility, as I was already beginning to suspect, was in fact due simply to your great-uncle's longing for an extinction as total and irreversible as possible of his capacity to think and remember.

Once again Dr Abramsky fell silent for a lengthy spell, occasionally scrutinizing the lines on his left hand. I believe, he then went on, looking up at me, I believe it was Fahnstock's unmistakably Austrian intonation that predisposed me towards him at first. He reminded me of my father, who was from Kolomea and, like Fahnstock, came from Galicia to the west after the dissolution of the Habsburg empire. Fahnstock tried to re-establish himself in his home town, Linz, whilst my father tried to start up in the liquor trade in Vienna, but both fell foul of circumstances, the one in Linz and the other in Vienna's Leopoldstadt. In early 1921 my father emigrated to America, and Fahnstock must have arrived in New York during the summer months, where he soon resumed his career in psychiatry. In 1925, following two years at the state hospital in Albany, he took up a position at Samaria, a newly established private sanatorium. At about the same time, my father died when a boiler exploded in a soda factory on the Lower East Side. After the accident, his body was found in a partly poached state. When I was growing up in Brooklyn I missed him very much. Even in the face of the greatest adversity he was confident; my mother, by contrast, seemed only a shadow after his death. I now think that, when I myself began as an assistant at the Samaria, I was uncritically on Fahnstock's side because much about him recalled my father. But when Fahnstock began to believe, towards the end of his career, that he had discovered a psychiatric miracle cure in the block or annihilation method, and when he, who had never had the slightest scientific ambition, increasingly became caught up in a kind of experimental mania and even planned to publish a paper about Ambrose, then, and only then, did it dawn on me that his fanatical interest as well as my own vacillation were, in the end, merely proof of our appalling ignorance and corruptibility.

It was almost evening. Dr Abramsky led me back through the arboretum to the drive. He was holding the white goose wing, and from time to time pointed the way ahead with it. Towards the end, he said as we walked, your great-uncle suffered progressive paralysis of the joints and limbs, probably caused by the shock therapy. After a while he had the greatest difficulty with everyday tasks. He took almost the whole day to get dressed. Simply to fasten his cufflinks and his bow tie took him hours. And he was hardly finished dressing but it was time to undress again. What was more, he was having constant trouble with his eyesight, and suffered from bad headaches, and so he often wore a green eyeshade – like someone who works in a gambling saloon. When I went to see him in his room on the last day of his life, because he had failed to appear for treatment for the first time, he was standing at the window, wearing the eyeshade, gazing out at the marshlands beyond the park. Oddly, he had put on armlets made of some satin-like material, such as he might have worn when he used to polish the silver. When I asked why he had not appeared at the appointed time, he replied (I remember his words exactly): It must have slipped my mind whilst I was waiting for the butterfly man. After he had made this enigmatic remark, Ambrose accompanied me without delay, down to the treatment room where Fahnstock was waiting, and submitted to all the preparations without the least resistance, as he always did. I see him lying before me, said Dr Abramsky, the electrodes on his temples, the rubber bit between his teeth, buckled into the canvas wraps that were riveted to the treatment table like a man shrouded for burial at sea. The session proceeded without incident. Fahnstock's prognosis was distinctly optimistic. But I could see from Ambrose's face that he was now destroyed, all but a vestige of him. When he came round from the anaesthetic, his eyes, which were now strangely glassy and fixed, clouded over, and a sigh that I can hear to this day rose from his breast. An orderly took him back to his room, and when I went there early the following morning, troubled by my conscience, I found him lying on his bed, in patent-leather boots, wearing full uniform, so to speak. Dr Abramsky walked the rest of the way beside me in silence. Nor did he say a word in farewell, but described a gentle arc with the goose wing in the darkening air.

In mid September 1991, when I travelled from England to Deauville during a dreadful drought, the season was long over, and even the Festival du Cinéma Américain, with which they tried to extend the more lucrative summer months a little, had come to its end. I cannot say whether I was expecting Deauville to have something special to offer – some remnant of the past, green avenues, beach promenades, or even a stylish or scandalous clientèle; whatever my notions may have been, it was immediately apparent that the once legendary resort, like everywhere else that one visits now, regardless of the country or continent, was hopelessly run down and ruined by traffic, shops and boutiques, and the insatiable urge for destruction. The villas built in the latter half of the nineteenth century, neo-Gothic castles with turrets and battlements, Swiss chalets, and even mock-oriental residences, were almost without exception a picture of neglect and desolation. If one pauses for a while before one of these seemingly unoccupied houses, as I did a number of times on my first morning walk through the streets of Deauville, one of the closed window shutters on the *parterre* or *bel étage* or the top floor, strange to relate, will open slightly, and a hand will appear and shake out a duster, fearfully slowly, so that soon one inevitably concludes that the whole of Deauville consists of gloomy interiors where womenfolk, condemned to perpetual invisibility and eternal dusting, move soundlessly about, waiting for the moment when they can signal with their dusters to some passer-by who has happened to stop outside their prison and stand gazing up. Almost everything, in fact, was shut, both in Deauville and across the river in Trouville – the Musée Montebello, the town archives in the town hall, the library (which I had planned to look around in), and even the children's day nursery *de l'enfant Jésus*, established through the generosity of

the long-deceased Madame la Baronne d'Erlanger, as I was informed by a commemorative plaque placed on the façade of the building by the grateful citizens of Deauville. Nor was the Grand Hôtel des Roches Noires open any more, a gigantic brick palace where American multimillionaires, English aristocrats, French high financiers and German industrialists basked in each other's company at the turn of the century. The Roches Noires, as far as I was able to

discover, had closed its doors in the Fifties or Sixties and was converted into apartments, though only those that had a sea view sold well. Now what was once the most luxurious hotel on the coast of Normandy is a monumental monstrosity half sunk in the sand. Most of the flats have long been empty, their owners having departed this life. But there are still some indestructible ladies who come every summer and haunt the immense edifice. They pull the white dustsheets off the furniture for a few weeks and at night, silent on their biers, they lie in the empty midst of it. They wander along the broad passageways, cross the huge reception rooms, climb and descend the echoing stairs, carefully placing one foot before the other, and in the early mornings they walk their ulcerous poodles and pekes on the promenade. In contrast to the Roches Noires, which is gradually falling down, the Hôtel Normandy at the other end of Trouville-Deauville, completed in 1912, is still an establishment of the finest class. Built around a number of courtyards in half-timber that looks at

once outsize and miniature, it is frequented nowadays almost exclusively by the Japanese, who are steered through the minutely prescribed daily programme by the hotel staff with an exquisite but also, as I observed, ice-cold courtesy verging on the indignant. And indeed, at the Normandy one felt one was not so much in a celebrated hotel of international standing as in a gastronomic pavilion built by the French for a world fair somewhere near Osaka, and I for one should not have been surprised in the slightest if I had walked out of the Normandy to find next to it another incongruous fantasy in the Balinese or Tyrolean style. Every three days the Japanese at the Normandy were exchanged for a new contingent of their countrymen, who, as one hotel guest explained to me, were brought direct, in air-conditioned coaches, from Charles de Gaulle airport to Deauville, the third call (after Las Vegas and Atlantic City) in a global gambling tour that took them on, back to Tokyo, via Vienna, Budapest and Macao. In Deauville, every morning at ten, they would troop over to the new casino, which was built at the same time as the Normandy, where they would play the machines till lunchtime, in arcades dense with flashing, kaleidoscopic lights and tootling garlands of sound. The afternoons and evenings were also spent at the machines, to which, with stoical faces, they sacrificed whole handfuls of coins; and like children on a spree they were delighted when at last a payout tinkled forth from the box. I never saw any of them at the roulette table. As midnight approached, only a few dubious clients from the provinces would be playing there, shady lawyers, estate agents or car dealers with their mistresses, trying to out-manoeuvre Fortune, who stood before them in the person of a stocky croupier clad inappropriately in the livery of a circus attendant in the big top. The roulette table, screened off with jade-green glass *paravents*, was in a recently refurbished inner hall – not, in other words, where players had gambled at Deauville in former times. I knew that in those days the gaming hall was much larger. Then there had been two rows of roulette and baccarat tables as well as tables where one could bet on little horses that kept running round and round in circles. Chandeliers of Venetian glass hung from the stuccoed ceiling, and through a dozen eight-metre-high half-rounded windows one looked out onto a terrace where the most exotic of personages would be gathered, in couples or groups; and beyond the balustrade, in the light that fell from the casino, one could see the white sands and, far out, the ocean-going yachts and small steamers, lit up and riding at anchor, beaming their Aldis lamps into the night sky, and little boats moving to and fro like slow glow-worms between them and the coast. When I first set foot in the casino at Deauville, the old gaming hall was filled with the last glimmer of evening light. Tables had been laid for a good hundred people, for a wedding banquet or some anniversary celebration. The rays of the setting sun were caught by the glasses and glinted on the silver drums of the band that was just beginning to rehearse for their gig. The instrumentalists were curly-haired and no longer the youngest. The songs they played dated from the Sixties, songs I heard countless times in the Union bar in Manchester. *It is the evening of the day.* The vocalist, a blonde girl with a voice still distinctly child-like, breathed passionately into the microphone, which she held up close to her lips with both hands. She was singing in English, though with a pronounced French accent. *It is the evening of the day, I sit and watch the children play.* At times, when she could not remember the proper words, her singing would become an ethereal hum. I sat down in one of the white lacquer chairs. The music filled the whole room. Pink puffy clouds right up to the golden arabesques of the ceiling stucco. "A whiter shade of pale."

Later that night, in my hotel room, I listened to the sound of the sea. I dreamt I was crossing the Atlantic in a *paquebot* whose deck superstructure looked exactly like the Hôtel Normandy. I was standing at the rail as we entered Le Havre at dawn. The foghorn boomed three times and the immense ship trembled beneath my feet. From Le Havre to Deauville I took the train. In my compartment there was a woman wearing a feathered hat, with a large variety of hatboxes. She was smoking a large Havanna cigar, and gazed tauntingly across at me through the blue haze from time to time. But I did not know how to address her, and in my embarrassment I sat staring at the white kid gloves, with their many tiny buttons, that lay beside her on the upholstered seat. Once I had reached Deauville I took a fly to the Hôtel des Roches Noires. The streets were inordinately busy: coaches and carriages of every kind, cars, handcarts, bicycles, errand boys, delivery men and *flâneurs* wove their seemingly aimless way. It was as if all pandemonium had broken loose. The hotel was hopelessly overbooked. Crowds of people were jostling at the reception desk. It was just before the start of the racing season, and everyone was determined to lodge at one of the best addresses, whatever the cost. Those who were staying at the Roches Noires hired sofas or armchairs to sleep on in the reading room or the salon; the staff were evacuated from their attic quarters to the cellar; the gentlemen ceded their beds to the ladies and lay where they could, in the foyer or the corridors, the window bays or landings, and on the billiard tables. By paying a horrendous bribe I secured a bunk in a lumber room, high on the wall like a luggage rack. Only when I was too fatigued to go on did I climb up into it and sleep for an hour or so. The rest of the time I was looking for Cosmo and Ambros night and day. Now and then I thought I saw them disappear into an entry or a lift or turn a street corner. Or else I really did see them, taking tea out in the courtyard, or in the hall leafing through the latest papers, which were brought early every morning at breakneck speed from Paris to Deauville by Gabriel the chauffeur. They were silent, as the dead usually are when they appear in our dreams, and seemed somewhat downcast and dejected. Generally, in fact, they behaved as if their altered condition, so to speak, were a terrible family secret not to be revealed under any circumstances. If I approached them, they dissolved before my very eyes, leaving behind them nothing but the vacant space they had occupied. Whenever I caught sight of them, I contented myself with observing them from a distance. Wherever I happened upon them it was as if they constituted a point of stillness in the ceaseless bustle. It seemed as though the whole world had gathered there in Deauville for the summer of 1913. I saw the Comtesse de Montgomery, the Comtesse de FitzJames, Baronne d'Erlanger and the Marquise de Massa, the Rothschilds, the Deutsch de la Meurthes, the Koechlins and Bürgels, the Peugeots, the Wormses and the Hennessys, the Isvolskys and the Orlovs, artistes of both sexes, fast women like Réjane and Reichenberg, Greek shipping tycoons, Mexican petroleum magnates and cotton planters from Louisiana. The *Trouville Gazette* reported that a veritable wave of the exotic had broken upon Deauville that year: *des musulmans moldo-valaques, des brahmanes hindous et toutes les variétés de Cafres, de Papous, de Niam-Niams et de Bachibouzouks importés en Europe avec leurs danses simiesques et leurs instruments sauvages.* Things were happening round the clock. At the first big race of the season, at La Touque hippodrome, I heard an English gossip columnist say: It actually seems as though people have learnt to sleep on the hoof. It's their glazed look that gives them away. Touch them, and they keel over. Dead tired myself, I stood on the grandstand of the hippodrome. The grass track around the polo field was bordered by long rows of poplars. Through my binoculars I could see their leaves turning in the breeze, silvery grey. The crowd was growing by the minute. Soon there was one vast sea of hats swelling below me, the white egret feathers cresting them like crowns of foam on waves that ebb darkly away. The loveliest of the young ladies appeared last of all, the yearlings of the season, as it were, wearing lace dresses through which their silken undergarments gleamed in Nile green, crevette, or absinthe blue. In no time at all they were surrounded by men in black, the most raffish of whom raised their top hats aloft on their canes. When the race was already due to have started, the Maharajah of Kashmir arrived in his Rolls, which was gold-plated within, and behind him a second limousine from which an incredibly obese lady alighted and was led to her seat by two ancient grooms. Immediately above her, I suddenly realized, were sitting Cosmo Solomon and Ambros. Ambros was wearing a buff linen suit and a black-lacquered Spanish straw hat on his head. But Cosmo was clad in a thick fleeced coat, despite the cloudless midsummer weather, and an aviator's cap from which his blond curls escaped. His right arm, resting on the back of Ambros's seat, was motionless, and motionless they both gazed into the distance. Otherwise, as I now recall, my dreams in Deauville were filled with constant whisperings of the rumours that were in circulation concerning Cosmo and Ambros. On one occasion I saw the two young men sitting late in the evening in the Normandy's vast dining hall at a small table of their own, placed especially for them in the centre of the room, apart from all the rest. On a silver platter between them, occasionally making slow movements, lay a lobster, gleaming a wonderful pink in the muted atmosphere. Ambros was steadily taking the lobster apart, with great skill, placing little morsels before Cosmo, who ate them like a well brought up child. The diners swayed as if there were a light swell, and only the women's glittering earrings and necklaces and the gentlemen's white shirt-fronts were to be seen. Nonetheless, I sensed that everyone kept their eyes on the two lobster eaters, whom I heard variously described as master and man, two friends, relatives, or even brothers. Endlessly the pros and cons of all these theories were advanced, and the discussions filled the hall with a low murmur, even long after the table for two had been cleared and the first light of dawn was at the windows. No doubt it was above all the eccentricity of Cosmo, combined with the impeccable manners of Ambros, that had aroused the curiosity of the Deauville summer guests. And their curiosity naturally grew, and the suspicions that were voiced waxed more audacious, the more the two friends contented themselves with each other's company, turning down the invitations that were extended to them daily. The astounding eloquence of Ambros, which contrasted so strikingly with Cosmo's seemingly total lack of words, also prompted speculation. Moreover, Cosmo's aerobatics and escapades on the polo field afforded a continual talking point, and the interest people took in the curious Americans reached its climax when Cosmo's unparalleled streak of luck began, in the *séparée* of the casino. Word of it spread through Deauville like wildfire. On top of the whispers already in circulation there was now added the rumour of fraud, or crooked dealing; and talk – on that evening in the dining room, too – never tired of suggesting that Ambros, who did not sit at the roulette table himself, but was always standing immediately behind Cosmo, possessed the mysterious powers of a *magnetiseur*. Indeed, he was so unfathomable that I felt that he could be compared only to the Austrian countess, a *femme au passé obscur* who held court in the somewhat remoter corners of my Deauville dream world. Exceptionally delicately built, and indeed almost transparent, she wore grey or brown moiré silk dresses, and would be besieged at any time of the day or night by a horde of admirers of either sex. No one knew her real name (there was no such person as Gräfin Dembowski in Vienna), nor could anyone estimate her age or say if she were married or not, or a widow. I first noticed Gräfin Dembowski when she did something that no woman had dared to do before her: she removed her white sun hat on the terrace of the casino and laid it on the balustrade beside her. And I saw her for the last time when, awakened from my Deauville dream, I went to the window of my hotel room. Morning was breaking. The beach still merged colourless into the sea, the sea into the sky. And there she was, in the pale but growing light of daybreak, on the deserted Promenade des Planches. Dressed in the most tasteless of styles and appallingly made up, there she came, with a white Angora rabbit lolloping along on a lead. She was also attended by a clubman in acid green livery, who would stoop down whenever the rabbit refused to go on and feed it a little of the enormous cauliflower he held in his crook'd left arm.

On the desk in front of me is the agenda book that belonged to Ambros, which Aunt Fini gave me on my winter visit to Cedar Glen West. It is a pocket diary for the year 1913, bound in soft burgundy leather and measuring about twelve centimetres by eight. Ambros must have bought it in Milan, because that is where his entries begin, on the 20th of August: Palace H, 3 pm, Signora M. Evening, Teatro S. Martino, Corso V. Em. *I tre Emisferi.* Deciphering his tiny handwriting, which not infrequently moved to and fro between several

AGENDA

languages, was an arduous task, one I should probably never have accomplished if those words committed to paper almost eighty years before had not, as it were, opened up of their own accord. The entries gradually become more detailed, and it appears that, at the end of August, Ambros and Cosmo left from Venice for Greece and Constantinople, in a steam yacht. Early morning (it says), myself on deck for a long time, looking astern. The lights of the city receding into the distance under a veil of rain. The islands in the lagoon like shadows. *Mal du pays. Le navigateur écrit son journal à la vue de la terre qui s'éloigne.* The following day he writes: Off the Croatian coast. Cosmo very restless. A beautiful sky. Treeless mountains. The clouds built high. As good as dark at three in the afternoon. Bad weather. We strike our sails. Seven in the evening, the storm full force. Waves breaking on the deck. The Austrian captain has lit an oil lamp before the picture of Our Lady in his cabin. He is kneeling on the floor, praying. In Italian, strange to say, for the poor lost seamen *sepolti in questo sacro mare.* The stormy night is followed by a windless day. Steam up, steadily southward. I put things back in order. In the failing light ahead, pearly grey on the line of the horizon, an island. Cosmo stands fore like a pilot. Calls the name Fano to a sailor. Sísiorsí, the sailor shouts, and, pointing ahead, he repeats, louder: Fano! Fano! Later, low on the already darkened island, I see a fire. There are fishermen on the beach. One of them waves a burning piece of wood. We pass them, and a few hours later enter the harbour of Kassiopé on the north coast of Kérkyra. Next morning the most fearful racket on board. Repairing damage to the engine. Ashore with Cosmo. Up to the ruins of the fortifications. A holm oak growing right out of the castle. We lie beneath the canopy of leaves as in an arbour. Below, they are hammering away at the boiler. A day out of time. At night we sleep on deck. The singing of crickets. Woken by a breeze on my brow. Across the straits, beyond the blue-black mountains of Albania, day is breaking, its glowing flame blazing across the lightless world. And at the same time two white ocean-going yachts trailing white smoke cross the scene, so slowly it is as if they were being pulled across a stage inch by inch. One would hardly think they were moving, but at length they are gone, into the wings of Cape Varvara with its dark green forests, over which hangs the thin sickle of the crescent moon. – 6th September: From Kérkyra via Ithaca and Patras into the Gulf of Corinth. At Itéa decided to send the boat on ahead and travel overland to Athens. Now in the hills at Delphi, the night already very cool. We lay down to sleep two hours ago, wrapped in our coats. Our saddles serve as pillows. The horses stand heads bowed beneath the laurel tree, the leaves of which rustle softly like tiny sheets of metal. Above us the Milky Way (where the Gods pass, says Cosmo), so resplendent that I can write this by its light. If I look straight up I can see the Swan and Cassiopeia. They are the same stars I saw above the Alps as a child and later above the Japanese house in its lake, above the Pacific, and out over Long Island Sound. I can scarcely believe I am the same person, and in Greece. But now and then the fragrance of juniper wafts across to us, so it is surely so.

After these nocturnal entries, the next of any length was written on the day they arrived in Constantinople. Yesterday morning left Piraeus, Ambros recorded on the 15th of September. Somewhat the worse for wear, he wrote, after the laborious overland journey. Calm voyage. Resting for hours under the awning on deck. Never seen water as blue. Truly ultramarine. This morning through the Dardanelles. Great flocks of cormorants. In the early afternoon, far ahead, the capital of the Orient appeared, like a mirage at first, then the green of trees and the colourful jostling houses gradually becoming more distinct. The masts of ships, crowding and swaying gently in a breeze, and the minarets, seeming to sway a little as well. – The Trieste captain paid, we take rooms at the Pera Palas for the time being. We enter the lobby as afternoon tea is being served. Cosmo writes in the register: *Frères Solomon, New York, en route pour la Chine. Pera*, the reception clerk tells me when I enquire, *pera* means beyond. Beyond Stamboul. Mellow orchestral music drifts through the foyer. Behind the drawn tulle curtains of the ballroom glide the shadows of dancing couples. *Quand l'amour meurt*, sings a woman, her voice meandering eerily. The stairs and rooms magnificent. Carpeted landscapes beneath high ceilings. Immense tubs in the bathrooms. From the balcony, a view across the Golden Horn. Evening falls. We watch the dark descending from the outlying hills upon the low roofs, rising from the depths of the city atop the lead-grey cupolas of the mosques till at length it reaches to the tips of the minarets, which gleam especially brightly one last time before the light goes. – At this point, Ambros's entries continue regardless of the dates in his diary. No one, he writes, could conceive of such a city. So many different kinds of buildings, so many different greens. The crowns of pines high aloft. Acacias, cork oaks, sycamores, eucalypts, junipers, laurels, a paradise of trees, shady slopes and groves with tumbling streams and springs. Every walk full of surprises, and indeed of alarm. The prospects change like the scenes in a play. One street lined with palatial buildings ends at a ravine. You go to a theatre and a door in the foyer opens into a copse; another time, you turn down a gloomy back street that narrows and narrows till you think you are trapped, whereupon you take one last desperate turn round a corner and find yourself suddenly gazing from a vantage point across the vastest of panoramas. You climb a bare hillside forever and find yourself once more in a shady valley, enter a house gate and are in the street, drift with the bustle in the bazaar and are suddenly amidst gravestones. For, like Death itself, the cemeteries of Constantinople are in the midst of life. For every one who departs this life, they say, a cypress is planted. In their dense branches the turtle doves nest. When night falls they stop cooing and partake of the silence of the dead. Once the silence descends, the bats come out and flit along their ways. Cosmo claims he can hear every one of their cries. – Whole districts of the city built entirely of wood. Houses of brown and grey weather-worn boards and planks, with flat-topped saddleback roofs and balconies. The Jewish quarter is built the same way. Walking through it today, we turn a corner and unexpectedly have a distant view of a blue line of mountains and the snowy summit of Olympus. For one awful heartbeat I imagine myself in Switzerland or at home again . . .

Have found a house out of the city, at Eyüp. It is next to the old village mosque, at the head of a square where three roads meet. In the middle of the paved square, with its pollard plane trees, the circular white marble basin of a fountain. Many people from the country pause here on their way to the city. Peasants with baskets of vegetables, charcoal burners, gypsies, tightrope walkers and bear trainers. I am surprised to see hardly a single wagon or any other vehicle. Everyone goes on

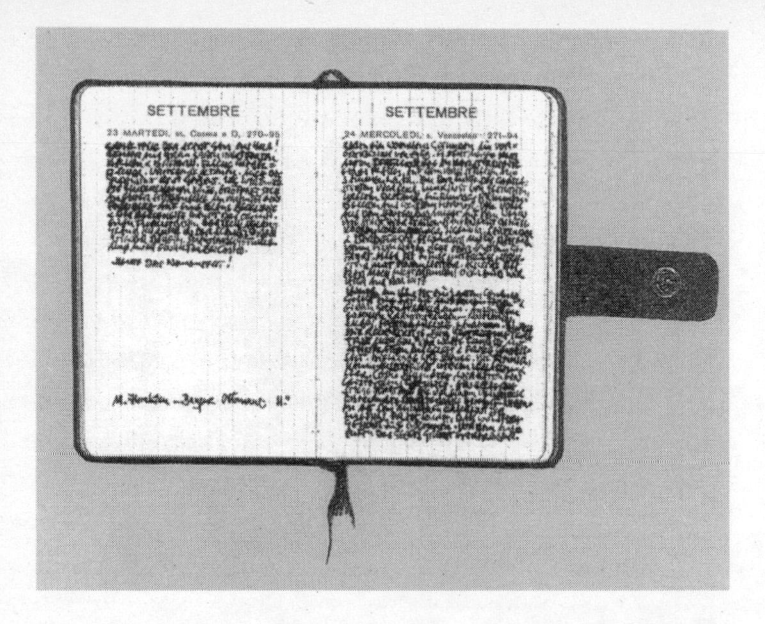

foot, or at best on a beast of burden. As if the wheel had not yet been invented. Or are we no longer a part of time? What meaning has a date like the 24th of September?? – Behind the house is a garden, or rather a kind of yard with a fig and a pomegranate tree. Herbs also grow there – rosemary, sage, myrtle, balm. Laudanum. One enters by the blue-painted door at the rear. The hall is broad and stone-flagged and newly whitewashed. The walls like snow. The rooms are almost bare of fittings, and make an empty, deserted impression. Cosmo claims we have rented a ghost house. Wooden steps lead up to a rooftop terrace shaded by an ancient vine. Next door, on the gallery of the minaret, a dwarfish muezzin appears. He is so close that we can see the features of his face. Before crying out the prayer, he calls a greeting across to us. – Under the rooftop vine, the first evening meal in our house. Below on the Golden Horn we can see thousands of boats crossing to and fro, and further to the right the city of Istanbul stretches to the horizon. Mounds of cloud above it, flame-red, copper and purple, lit by the setting sun. Near daybreak we hear a sound that fills the air, such as we have never heard before, a sound like the whispering of a far-off multitude gathered in the open in a field or on a mountain-side. We go up to the roof and see a moving baldachin, a pattern of black and white canopied overhead as far as the eye can see. Countless storks, migrating south. Later in the morning we still talk about them in a coffee house on the shore of the Horn. We are sitting on an open balcony at some height, on show like two saints. Tall schooners pass by, at no distance at all. One can feel the swathes of air as they go. In stormy weather, the proprietor says, their booms sometimes smash a window or knock plants off ledges. – 17th October: behind with my notes, less through the demands of life than through idleness. Yesterday an excursion in a Turkish boat, down the Golden Horn and then along the right, Asian bank of the Bosphorus. We leave the outer parts of the city behind. Forested crags, embankments with evergreens. Here and there, lone villas and white summerhouses. Cosmo proves a good sailor. At one point we are surrounded by I do not know how many dolphins. There must have been hundreds, if not thousands. Like a great herd of swine they ploughed the waves with their muzzles and circled us time and again before finally plunging head over tail away. In the deep coves, the branches bent down low to the eddying waters. We slipped through beneath the trees and, with just a few pulls on the oars, entered a harbour surrounded by strangely silent houses. Two men were squatting on the quay playing dice. Otherwise there was not a soul about. We entered the little mosque by the gate. In an alcove in the half-light within sat a young man studying the Koran. His lids were half closed, his lips were murmuring softly. His body was rocking to and fro. In the middle of the hall a husbandman was saying his afternoon prayers. Again and again he touched his forehead to the floor and remained bowed down for what seemed to me an eternity. The soles of his feet gleamed in the straggling light that entered through the doorway. At length he stood up, first casting a deferential glance to right and left, over his shoulders – to greet his guardian angels, who stand behind him, said Cosmo. We turned to go, from the half-dark of the mosque into the sand-white brightness of the harbour square. As we crossed it, both shading our dazzled eyes like desert travellers, a grey pigeon about the size of a full-grown cockerel tottered clumsily ahead of us, leading us to an alley where we came across a dervish aged about twelve. He was wearing a

very wide gown that reached to the ground and a close-fitting jacket made, like the gown, of the finest linen. The boy, who was extraordinarily beautiful, was wearing a high brimless camel-hair toque on his head. I spoke to him in Turkish, but he only looked at us without a word. On the return, our boat seemed to glide of itself along the dark green overhung crags. The sun had set, the water was a shadowy plain, but higher up a light still moved here and there. Cosmo, at the tiller, says he wants to come out shortly once again, with a photographer, to take a souvenir photograph of the boy dervish . . .

On the 26th of October Ambros writes: Collected the photographs of the white boy from the studio today. Later, made enquiries at the Chemins de Fer Orientaux and the Banque Ottomane concerning our onward journey. Also bought a Turkish costume for Cosmo and one for myself. Spent the evening with timetables, maps and Karl Baedeker's handbook.

The route they took from Constantinople can be followed fairly closely from the diary notes, despite the fact that they are farther apart now, and at times stop altogether.

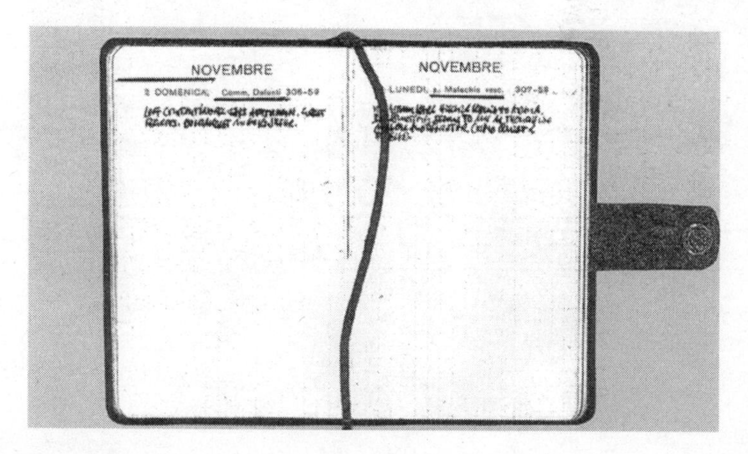

They must have crossed the whole of Turkey by rail, down to Adana, and gone on from there to Aleppo and Beirut, and seem to have spent the best part of a fortnight in the Lebanon, for it is not till the 21st of November that "passage to Jaffa" is entered. The day they arrived in Jaffa, through an agent at Franks Hotel, Dr Immanuel Benzinger, they hired two horses at a cost of 15 francs each for the twelve-hour ride up from the coast to Jerusalem. The luggage went ahead by rail. Early on the morning of the 25th, Cosmo and Ambros were on their way through the orange groves and on, in a southeasterly direction, across the plain of Sharon and towards the mountains of Judaea. Through the Holy Land, writes Ambros, often far off the track. The rocks all around radiantly white in the light. For long stretches not a tree, not a shrub, scarcely so much as a meagre clump of weeds. Cosmo very taciturn. Darkened sky. Great clouds of dust rolling through the air. Terrible desolation and emptiness. Late in the afternoon it cleared once more. A rosy glow lay upon the valley, and through an opening in the mountainous terrain we could see the promised city in the distance – a ruined and broken mass of rocks, the Queen of the desert . . . An hour after nightfall we ride into the courtyard of the Hotel Kaminitz on the Jaffa Road. The maître d'hôtel, a pomaded little Frenchman, is utterly astounded, indeed *scandalisé*, to see these dust-caked new arrivals, and shakes his head as he studies our entry in the register. Not until I ask him to see that our horses are properly looked after does he recall his duties, whereupon he deals with everything as fast as he is able. The rooms are furnished in a most peculiar manner. One cannot say what period or part of the world one is in. View to one side across domed stone rooftops. In the white moonlight they resemble a frozen sea. Deep weariness, sleep till well into the morning. Numerous dreams with strange voices and shouts. At noontime a deathly silence, broken only by the eternal crowing of cocks. – Today (it reads two days later) a first walk through the city and into the outer districts. All in all, a frightful impression. Vendors of souvenirs and devotional objects in almost every building. They crouch in the gloom of their shops amidst hundreds of olivewood carvings and junk decorated with mother-of-pearl. From the end of the month the faithful will be coming to buy, hordes of them, ten or fifteen thousand Christian pilgrims from all around the world. The more recent buildings of an ugliness hard to describe. Large quantities of filth in the streets. *On marche sur des merdes!!!* Pulverized limestone ankle-deep in places. The few plants which have survived the drought that has lasted since May are covered in this powdery meal as if by a blight. *Une malédiction semble planer sur la ville.* Decay, nothing but decay, marasmus and emptiness. Not a sign of any business or industry. All we passed were a tallow-and-soap factory and a bone-and-hide works. Next to this, in a wide square, the knacker's yard. In the middle a big hole. Coagulated blood, heaps of entrails, blackish-brown tripes, dried and scorched by the sun . . . Otherwise one church after another, monasteries, religious and philanthropic establishments of every kind and denomination. On the northerly side are the Russian cathedral, the Russian Men's and Women's hospice, the French Hôpital de St Louis, the Jewish Home for the Blind, the Church and Hospice of St Augustine, the German school, the German Orphanage, the German Asylum for the Deaf and Dumb, the School of the London Mission to the Jews, the Abyssinian Church, the Anglican Church, College and Bishop's House, the Dominican Friary, the Seminary and Basilica of St Stephen, the Rothschild Girls' Institute, the Alliance Israélite College of Commerce, the Church of Notre Dame de France, and, beside the pool of Bethesda, the Monastery of St Anne; on the Mount of Olives are the Russian Tower, the Church of the Assumption, the French Church of Pater Noster, the Carmelite nunnery, the building that houses the Empress Augusta Victoria Foundation, the Russian Orthodox Church of Mary Magdalene, and the

Church of Agony; to the south and west are the Armenian Orthodox Monastery of Mount Zion, the Protestant School, the Sisters of St Vincent, the Hospice of the Knights of St John, the Convent of the Sisters of St Clare, the Montefiore Hospice and the Moravian Lepers' Home. In the centre of the city there are the Church and Residence of the Latin Patriarch, the Dome of the Rock, the School of the Frères de la Doctrine Chrétienne, the school and printing works of the Franciscan Brotherhood, the Coptic Monastery, the German

Hospice, the German Protestant Church of the Redeemer, the United Armenian Church of the Spasm (as it is called), the Couvent des Soeurs de Zion, the Austrian Hospital, the Monastery and Seminary of the Algerian Mission Brotherhood, the Church of Sant'Anna, the Jewish Hospice, the Ashkenazy and Sephardic Synagogues, and the Church of the Holy Sepulchre, below the portal of which a misshapen little man with a cucumber of a nose offered us his services as a guide through the intricacies of the aisles and transepts, chapels, shrines and altars. He was wearing a bright yellow frock coat which to my mind dated far back into the last century, and his crooked legs were clad in what had once been a dragoon's breeches, with sky-blue piping. Taking tiny steps, always half turned to us, he danced ahead and talked nonstop in a language he probably thought to be German or English but which was in fact of his own invention and to me, at all events, quite incomprehensible. Whenever his eye fell on me I felt as despised and cold as a stray dog. Later, too, outside the Church of the Holy Sepulchre, a continuing feeling of oppressiveness and misery. No matter which direction we went in, we always came up at one of the steep ravines that crisscross the city, falling away to the valleys. By now the ravines have largely been filled with the rubbish of a thousand years, and everywhere liquid waste flows openly into them. As a result, the water of numerous springs has become undrinkable. The erstwhile pools of Siloam are no more than foul puddles and cesspits, a morass from which the miasma rises that causes epidemics to rage here almost every summer. Cosmo says repeatedly that he is utterly horrified by the city.

On the 27th of November Ambros notes that he has been to Raad's Photographic Studio in the Jaffa Road and has had his picture taken, at Cosmo's wish, in his new striped Arab robe. In the afternoon (he continues) out of the city to the Mount of Olives. We pass a withered vineyard. The soil beneath the black vines rust-coloured, exhausted and scorched. Scarcely a wild olive tree, a thorn bush, or a little hyssop. On the crest of the Mount of Olives runs a riding track. Beyond the valley of Jehoshaphat, where at the end of time, it is said, the entire human race will gather in the flesh, the silent city rises from the white limestone with its domes, towers and ruins. Over the rooftops not a sound, not a trace of smoke, nothing. Nowhere, as far as the eye can see, is there any sign of life, not an animal scurrying by, or even the smallest bird in flight. *On dirait que c'est la terre maudite . . .* On the other side, what must be more than three thousand feet below, the Jordan and part of the Dead Sea. The air is so bright, so thin and so clear that without thinking one might reach out a hand to touch the tamarisks down there on the river bank. Never before had we been washed in such a flood of light! A little further on, we found a place to rest in a mountain hollow where a stunted box tree and a few wormwood shrubs grow. We leant against the rock wall for a long time, feeling how everything gradually faded . . . In the evening, studied the guidebook I bought in Paris. In the past, it says, Jerusalem looked quite different. Nine tenths of the splendours of the world were to be found in this magnificent city. Desert caravans brought spices, precious stones, silk and gold. From the sea ports of Jaffa and Askalon, merchandise came up in abundance. The arts and commerce were in full flower. Before the walls, carefully tended gardens lay outspread, the valley of Jehoshaphat was canopied with cedars, there were streams, springs, fish pools, deep channels, and everywhere cool shade. And then came the age of destruction. Every settlement up to a four-hour journey away in every direction was destroyed, the irrigation systems were wrecked, and the trees and bushes were cut down, burnt and blasted, down to the very last stump. For years the Caesars deliberately made it impossible to live there, and in later times too Jerusalem was repeatedly attacked, liberated and pacified, until at last the desolation was complete and nothing remained of the matchless wealth of the Promised Land but dry stone and a remote idea in the heads of its people, now dispersed throughout the world.

4th December: Last night dreamt that Cosmo and I crossed the glaring emptiness of the Jordan valley. A blind guide walks ahead of us. He points his staff to a dark spot on the horizon and cries out, several times, *er-Riha, er-Riha.* As we approach, er-Riha proves to be a dirty village with sand and dust swirling about it. The entire population has gathered on the edge of the village in the shade of a tumbledown sugar mill. One has the impression that they are nothing but beggars and footpads. A noticeable number are gouty, hunch-backed or disfigured. Others are lepers or have immense goitres. Now I see that all these people are from Gopprechts. Our Arab escorts fire their long rifles into the air. We ride past, and the people cast malevolent looks after us. At the foot of a low hill we pitch the black tents. The Arabs light a small fire and cook a dark green broth of Jew's mallow and mint leaves, and bring some of it over to us in tin bowls, with slices of lemon and crushed grain. Night falls rapidly. Cosmo lights the lamp and spreads out his map on the colourful carpet. He points to one of the many white spaces and says: We are now in Jericho. The oasis is a four-hour walk in length and a one-hour walk in breadth, and of a rare beauty perhaps matched only by the paradisal orchard of Damascus – *le merveilleux verger de Damas.* The people here have all they want. Whatever they sow grows immediately in this soft, fertile soil. The glorious gardens flower forever. The greening corn sways in the bright palm groves. The fiery heat of summer is made bearable by the many watercourses and pastures, the crowns of the trees and the vine leaves over the pathways. The winters are so mild that the people of this blessèd land wear no more than a linen shirt, even when the mountains of Judaea, not far off, are white with snow. – Several blank pages follow the account of the dream of er-Riha. During this time, Ambros must have been chiefly occupied with recruiting a small troop of Arabs and acquiring the equipment and provisions needed for an expedition to the Dead Sea, for on the 16th of December he writes: Left over-crowded Jerusalem with its hordes of pilgrims three days ago and rode down the Kidron Valley into the lowest region on earth. Then, at the foot of the Yeshimon Mountains, along the Sea as far as Ain Jidy. One wrongly imagines these shores as destroyed by fire and brimstone, a thing of salt and ashes for thousands of years. I myself have heard the Dead Sea, which is about the size of Lac Leman, described as being as motionless as molten lead, though the surface is ruffled at times into a phosphorescent foam. Birds cannot fly across it, they say, without suffocating in the air, and others report that on moonlit nights an aura of the grave, the colour of absinthe, rises from its depths. None of all this have we found to be true. In fact, the Sea's waters are wonderfully clear, and break on the shore with scarcely a sound. On the high ground to the right there are green clefts from which streams come forth.

There is also to be seen a mysterious white line that is visible early in the morning. It runs the length of the Sea, and vanishes an hour or so later. No one, thus Ibrahim Hishmeh, our Arab guide, can explain it or give a reason. Ain Jidy itself is a blessèd spot with pure spring water and rich vegetation. We made our camp by some bushes on the shore where snipe stalk and the bulbul bird, brown and blue of plumage and red of beak, sings. Yesterday I thought I saw a large dark hare, and a butterfly with gold-speckled wings. In the evening, when we were sitting on the shore, Cosmo said that once the whole of the land of Zoar on the south bank was like this. Where now mere traces remained of the five overthrown cities of Gomorrha, Ruma, Sodom, Seadeh and Seboah, the oleanders once grew thirty feet high beside rivers that never ran dry, and there were acacia forests and oshac trees as in Florida. There were irrigated orchards and melon fields far and wide, and he had read a passage where Lynch, the explorer, claimed that down from the gorge of Wadi Kerek a forest torrent fell with a fearful roar that could only be compared with the Niagara Falls. – In the third night of our stay at Ain Jidy a stiff wind rose out on the Sea and stirred the heavy waters. On land it was calmer. The Arabs had long been asleep beside the horses. I was still sitting up in our bed, which was open to the heavens, in the light of the swaying lantern. Cosmo, curled up slightly, was sleeping at my side. Suddenly a quail, perhaps frightened by the storm on the Sea, took refuge in his lap and remained there, calm now, as if it were its rightful place. But at daybreak, when Cosmo stirred, it ran away quickly across the level ground, as quail do, lifted off into the air, beat its wings tremendously fast for a moment, then extended them rigid and motionless and glided by a little thicket in an utterly beautiful curve, and was gone. It was shortly before sunrise. Across the water, about twelve miles away, the blue-black ridge-line of the Moab Mountains of Araby ran level along the horizon, merely rising or dipping slightly at points, so that one might have thought the watercolourist's hand had trembled a little.

The last entry in my Great-Uncle Adelwarth's little agenda book was written on the Feast of Stephen. Cosmo, it reads, had had a bad fever after their return to Jerusalem but was already on the way to recovery again. My great-uncle also noted that late the previous afternoon it had begun to snow and that, looking out of the hotel window at the city, white in the falling dusk, it made him think of times long gone. Memory, he added in a postscript, often strikes me as a kind of dumbness. It makes one's head heavy and giddy, as if one were not looking back down the receding perspectives of time but rather down on the earth from a great height, from one of those towers whose tops are lost to view in the clouds.

MAX FERBER

They come when night falls
to search for life

Until my twenty-second year I had never been further away from home than a five- or six-hour train journey, and it was because of this that in the autumn of 1966, when I decided, for various reasons, to move to England, I had a barely adequate notion of what the country was like or how, thrown back entirely on my own resources, I would fare abroad. It may have been partly due to my inexperience that I managed to weather the two-hour night flight from Kloten airport to Manchester without too many misgivings. There were only a very few passengers on board, and, as I recall, they sat wrapped up in their coats, far apart in the half-darkness of the cold body of the aircraft. Nowadays, when usually one is quite dreadfully crammed in together with one's fellow passengers, and aggravated by the unwanted attentions of the cabin crew, I am frequently beset with a scarcely containable fear of flying; but at that time, our even passage through the night skies filled me with a sense (false, as I now know) of security. Once we had crossed France and the Channel, sunk in darkness below, I gazed down lost in wonder at the network of lights that stretched from the southerly outskirts of London to the Midlands, their orange sodium glare the first sign that from now on I would be living in a different world. Not until we were approaching the Peak District south of Manchester did the strings of street lights gradually peter out into the dark. At the same time, from behind a bank of cloud that covered the entire horizon to the east, the disc of the moon rose, and by its pale glow the hills, peaks and ridges which had previously been invisible could be seen below us, like a vast, ice-grey sea moved by a great swell. With a grinding roar, its wings trembling, the aircraft toiled downwards until we passed by the strangely ribbed flank of a long, bare mountain ridge seemingly close enough to touch, and appearing to me to be rising and sinking like a giant recumbent body, heaving as it breathed. Looping round in one more curve, the roar of the engines steadily increasing, the plane set a course across open country. By now, we should have been able to make out the sprawling mass of Manchester, yet one could see nothing but a faint glimmer, as if from a fire almost suffocated in ash. A blanket of fog that had risen out of the marshy plains that reached as far as the Irish Sea had covered the city, a city spread across a thousand square kilometres, built of countless bricks and inhabited by millions of souls, dead and alive.

Although only a scant dozen passengers had disembarked at Ringway airport from the Zurich flight, it took almost an hour until our luggage emerged from the depths, and another hour until I had cleared customs: the officers, understandably bored at that time of the night, suddenly mustered an alarming degree of exactitude as they dealt with me, a rare case, in those days, of a student who planned to settle in Manchester to pursue research, bringing with him a variety of letters and papers of identification and recommendation. It was thus already five o'clock by the time I climbed into a taxi and headed for the city centre. In contrast to today, when a continental zeal for business has infected the British, in the Sixties no one was out and about in English cities so early in the morning. So, with only an occasional traffic light to delay us, we drove swiftly through the not unhandsome suburbs of Gatley, Northenden and Didsbury to Manchester itself. Day was just breaking, and I looked out in amazement at the rows of uniform houses, which seemed the more run-down the closer we got to the city centre. In Moss Side and Hulme there were whole blocks where the doors and windows were boarded up, and whole districts where everything had been demolished. Views opened up across the wasteland towards the still immensely impressive agglomeration of gigantic Victorian office blocks and warehouses, about a kilometre distant, that had once been the hub of one of the nineteenth century's miracle cities but, as I was soon to find out, was now almost hollow to the core. As we drove in among the dark ravines between the brick buildings, most of which were six or eight storeys high and sometimes adorned with glazed ceramic tiles, it turned out that even there, in the heart of the city, not a soul was to be seen, though by now it was almost a quarter to six. One might have supposed that the city had long since been deserted, and was left now as a necropolis or mausoleum. The taxi driver, whom I had asked to take me to a hotel that was (as I put it) not too expensive, gave me to understand that hotels of the kind I wanted were rare in the city centre, but after driving around a little he turned off Great Bridgewater Street into a narrow alleyway and pulled up at a house scarcely the width of two windows, on the soot-blackened front of which was the name AROSA in sweeping neon letters.

Just keep ringing, said the driver as he left. And I really

did have to push the bell long and repeatedly before there was a sign of movement within. After some rattling and shooting of bolts, the door was opened by a lady with curly blonde hair, perhaps not quite forty, with a generally wavy, Lorelei-like air about her. For a while we stood there in wordless confrontation, both of us with an expression of disbelief, myself beside my luggage and she in a pink dressing gown that was made of a material found only in the bedrooms of the English lower classes and is unaccountably called candlewick. Mrs Irlam – Yes, Irlam like Irlam in Manchester, I would later hear her saying down the phone time and again – Mrs Irlam broke the silence with a question that summed up both her jolted state, roused from her sleep, and her amusement at the sight of me: And where have you sprung from? – a question which she promptly answered herself, observing that only *an alien* would show up on her doorstep at such an hour on a blessed Friday morning with a case like that. But then, smiling enigmatically, Mrs Irlam turned back in, which I took as a sign to follow her. We went into a windowless room off the tiny hall, where a roll-top desk crammed to bursting with letters and documents, a mahogany chest stuffed with an assortment of bedclothes and candlewick bedspreads, an ancient wall telephone, a keyrack, and a large photograph of a pretty Salvation Army girl, in a black varnished frame, all had, it seemed to me, a life entirely of their own. The girl was in uniform, standing in front of an ivy-covered wall and holding a glistening flugelhorn in the crook of her arm. Inscribed on the slightly foxed *passe-partout*, in a flowing hand that leant heavily to one side, were the words: *Gracie Irlam, Urmston nr Manchester, 17 May 1944*. Third floor, she said, and, nodding across the hall, her eyebrows raised, added: the lift's over there. The lift was so tiny that I only just fitted in with my case, and its floor was so thin that it sagged beneath the weight of even a single passenger. Later I hardly used it, although it took me quite some time before I could find my way around the maze of dead-end corridors, emergency exits, doors to rooms, toilets and fire escapes, landings and staircases. The room that I moved into that morning, and did not move out of until the following spring, was carpeted in a large floral pattern, wallpapered with violets, and furnished with a wardrobe, a washstand, and an iron bedstead with a candlewick bedspread. From the window there was a view onto semi-derelict slate-roofed outbuildings below and a back yard where rats thronged all that autumn until, a week or so before Christmas, a little ratcatcher by the name of Renfield turned up several times with a battered bucket full of rat poison. He doled the poison out into various corners, drains and pipes, using a soup spoon tied to a short stick, and for a few months the number of rats was considerably reduced. If one looked out across the yard, rather than down into it, one saw the many-windowed deserted depot of the Great Northern Railway Company, a little way beyond a black canal, where sometimes lights would flit about erratically at night.

The day of my arrival at the Arosa, like most of the days, weeks and months to come, was a time of remarkable silence and emptiness. I spent the morning unpacking my suitcase and bags, stowing away my clothing and linen, and arranging my writing materials and other belongings; then, tired after a night of travelling, I fell asleep on my iron bed, my face buried in the candlewick bedspread, which smelled faintly of violet-scented soap. I did not come to till almost half past three, when Mrs Irlam knocked at my door. Apparently by way of a special welcome, she brought me, on a silver tray, an electric appliance of a kind I had never seen before. She explained that it was called a *teas-maid*, and was both an alarm clock and a tea-making machine. When I made tea and the

steam rose from it, the shiny stainless steel contraption on its ivory-coloured metal base looked like a miniature power plant, and the dial of the clock, as I soon found as dusk fell, glowed a phosphorescent lime green that I was familiar with from childhood and which I had always felt afforded me an unaccountable protection at night. That may be why it has often seemed, when I have thought back to those early days in Manchester, as if the tea maker brought to my room by Mrs Irlam, by Gracie – you must call me Gracie, she said – as if it was that weird and serviceable gadget, with its nocturnal glow, its muted morning bubbling, and its mere presence by day, that kept me holding on to life at a time when I felt a deep sense of isolation in which I might well have become completely submerged. Very useful, these are, said Gracie as she showed me how to operate the teas-maid that November afternoon; and she was right. After my initiation into the mysteries of what Gracie called an *electrical miracle*, we went on talking in a friendly fashion, and she repeatedly emphasized that her hotel was a quiet establishment, even if sometimes in the evenings there was (as she put it) a certain commotion. But that need not concern you. It's travelling gentlemen that come and go. And indeed, it was not until after office hours that the doors would open and the stairs creak at the Hotel Arosa, and one would encounter the gentlemen Gracie had referred to, bustling characters clad almost without exception in tattered gabardine coats or macs. Not until nearly eleven at night did the toings and froings cease and the garish women disappear – whom Gracie would refer to, without the slightest hint of irony, with a hold-all phrase she had evidently coined herself, as *the gentlemen's travelling companions.*

Every evening of the week, the Arosa was bustling with salesmen and clerks, but on Saturday evening, as in the entire rest of the city centre, there was no sign of life. Interrupted only occasionally by stray customers she called *irregulars*, Gracie would sit at the roll-top desk in her office doing the books. She did her best to smooth out the grey-green pound notes and brick-red ten-shilling notes, then laid them carefully in piles, and, whispering as if at some mystical rite, counted them until she had come up with the same total at least twice. She dealt with the coins no less meticulously; there was always a considerable quantity, and she stacked them in even columns of copper, brass and silver before she set about calculating the total, which she did partly by manual and partly by mathematical means, first converting the pennies, threepenny bits and sixpences to shillings and then the shillings, florins and half crowns into pounds. The final conversion that then followed, of the pound total thus arrived at into the guineas which were at that time still the customary unit in better business establishments, always proved the most difficult part of this financial operation, but without a doubt it was also its crowning glory. Gracie would enter the sum in guineas in her ledger, sign and date it, and stow the money in a Pickley & Patricroft safe that was built into the wall by the desk. On Sundays, she would invariably leave the house early in the morning, carrying a small patent leather case, only to return, just as unfailingly, at lunchtime on the Monday.

As for myself, on those Sundays in the utterly deserted hotel I would regularly be overcome by such a sense of aimlessness and futility that I would go out, purely in order to preserve an illusion of purpose, and walk about amidst the city's immense and time-blackened nineteenth-century buildings, with no particular destination in mind. On those wanderings, when winter light flooded the deserted streets and squares for the few rare hours of real daylight, I never ceased to be amazed by the completeness with which anthracite-coloured Manchester, the city from which industrialization had spread across the entire world, displayed the clearly chronic process of its impoverishment and degradation to anyone who cared to see. Even the grandest of the buildings, such as the Royal Exchange, the Refuge Assurance Company, the Grosvenor Picture Palace, and indeed the Piccadilly Plaza, which had been built only a few years before, seemed so empty and abandoned that one might have supposed oneself surrounded by mysterious façades or theatrical backdrops. Everything then would appear utterly unreal to me, on those sombre December days when dusk was already falling at three o'clock, when the starlings, which I had previously imagined to be migratory songbirds, descended upon the city in dark flocks that must have numbered hundreds of thousands, and, shrieking incessantly, settled close together on the ledges and copings of warehouses for the night.

Little by little my Sunday walks would take me beyond the city centre to districts in the immediate neighbourhood, such as the one-time Jewish quarter around the star-shaped complex of Strangeways prison, behind Victoria Station. This quarter had been a centre for Manchester's large Jewish community until the inter-war years, but those who lived there had moved into the suburbs and the district had meanwhile been demolished by order of the municipality. All I found still standing was one single row of empty houses, the wind blowing through the smashed windows and doors; and, by way of a sign that someone really had once been there, the barely decipherable brass plate of a one-time lawyers' office, bearing names that had a legendary ring to my ear: Glickmann, Grunwald and Gottgetreu. In Ardwick, Brunswick, All Saints, Hulme and Angel Fields too, districts adjoining the centre to the south, whole square kilometres of working-class homes had been pulled down by the authorities, so that, once the demolition rubble had been removed, all that was left to recall the lives of thousands of people was the grid-like layout of the streets. When night fell upon those vast spaces, which I came to think of as the Elysian Fields, fires would begin to flicker here and there and children would

stand around them or skip about, restless shadowy figures. On that bare terrain, which was like a glacis around the heart of the city, it was in fact always and only children that one encountered. They strayed in small groups, in gangs, or quite alone, as if they had nowhere that they could call home. I remember, for instance, late one November afternoon, when the white mist was already rising from the ground, coming across a little boy at a crossroads in the midst of the Angel Fields wasteland, with a Guy stuffed with old rags on a hand-cart: the only person out and about in the whole area, wanting a penny for his silent companion.

It was early the following year, if I remember correctly, that I ventured further out of the city, in a southwesterly direction, beyond St George and Ordsall, along the bank of the canal across which, from my window, I could see the Great Northern Railway Company depot. It was a bright, radiant day, and the water, a gleaming black in its embankment of massive masonry blocks, reflected the white clouds that scudded across the sky. It was so strangely silent that (as I now think I remember) I could hear sighs in the abandoned depots and warehouses, and was frightened to death when a number of seagulls, squawking stridently, all of a sudden flew

out of the shadow of one of the high buildings, into the light. I passed a long-disused gasworks, a coal depot, a bonemill, and what seemed the unending cast-iron palisade fence of the Ordsall slaughterhouse, a Gothic castle in liver-coloured brick, with parapets, battlements, and numerous turrets and gateways, the sight of which absurdly brought to my mind the name of Haeberlein & Metzger, the Nuremberg *Lebkuchen* makers; whereupon that name promptly stuck in my head, a bad joke of sorts, and continued to knock about there for the rest of the day. Three quarters of an hour later I reached the port of Manchester, where docks kilometres in length branched off the Ship Canal as it entered the city in a broad arc, forming wide side-arms and surfaces on which one could see nothing had moved for years. The few barges and freighters that lay far apart at the docksides, making an oddly broken impression, put me in mind of some massive shipping disaster. Not far from the locks at the harbour mouth, on a road that ran from the docks to Trafford Park, I came across a sign on which TO THE STUDIOS had been painted in crude brush-strokes. It pointed in to a cobbled yard in the middle of which, on a patch of grass, an almond tree was in blossom. At one time the yard must have been part of a carriage business, since it was enclosed partly by stables and outbuildings and partly by one- or two-storey buildings that had formerly been living quarters and office premises. In one of these seemingly deserted buildings was a studio which, in the months to come, I visited as often as I thought acceptable, to talk to the painter who had been working there since the late Forties, ten hours a day, the seventh day not excepted.

When one entered the studio it was a good while before one's eyes adjusted to the curious light, and, as one began to see again, it seemed as if everything in that space, which measured perhaps twelve metres by twelve and was impenetrable to the gaze, was slowly but surely moving in upon the middle. The darkness that had gathered in the corners, the puffy tidemarked plaster and the paint that flaked off the walls, the shelves overloaded with books and piles of newspapers, the boxes, work benches and side tables, the wing armchair, the gas cooker, the mattresses, the crammed mountains of papers, crockery and various materials, the paint pots gleaming carmine red, leaf green and lead white in the gloom, the blue flames of the two paraffin heaters: the entire furniture was advancing, millimetre by millimetre, upon the central space where Ferber had set up his easel in the grey light that entered through a high north-facing window layered with the dust of decades. Since he applied the paint thickly, and then repeatedly scratched it off the canvas as his work proceeded, the floor was covered with a largely hardened and encrusted deposit of droppings, mixed with coal dust, several centimetres thick at the centre and thinning out towards the outer edges, in places resembling the flow of lava. This, said Ferber, was the true product of his continuing endeavours and the most palpable proof of his failure. It had always been of the greatest importance to him, Ferber once remarked casually, that nothing should change at his place of work, that everything should remain as it was, as he had arranged it, and that nothing further should be added but the debris generated by painting and the dust that continuously fell and which, as he was coming to realize, he loved more than anything else in the world. He felt closer to dust, he said, than to light, air or water. There was nothing he found so unbearable as a well-dusted house, and he never felt more at home than in places where things remained undisturbed, muted under the grey, velvety sinter left when matter dissolved, little by little, into nothingness. And indeed, when I watched Ferber working on one of his portrait studies over a number of weeks, I often thought that his prime concern was to increase the dust. He drew with vigorous abandon, frequently going through half a dozen of his willow-wood charcoal sticks in the shortest of time; and that process of drawing and shading on the thick, leathery paper, as well as the concomitant business of constantly erasing what he had drawn with a woollen rag already heavy with charcoal, really amounted to nothing but a steady production of dust, which never ceased except at night. Time and again, at the end of a working day, I marvelled to see that Ferber, with the few lines and shadows that had escaped annihilation, had created a portrait of great vividness. And all the more did I marvel when, the following morning, the moment the model had sat down and he had taken a look at him or her, he would erase the portrait yet again, and once more set about excavating the features of his model, who by now was distinctly wearied by this manner of working, from a surface already badly damaged by the continual destruction. The facial features and eyes, said Ferber, remained ultimately unknowable for him. He might reject as many as forty variants, or smudge them back into the paper and overdraw new attempts upon them; and if he then decided that the portrait was done, not so much because he was convinced that it was finished as through sheer exhaustion, an onlooker might well feel that it had evolved from a long lineage of grey, ancestral faces, rendered unto ash but still there, as ghostly presences, on the harried paper.

As a rule, Ferber spent the mornings before he began work, and the evenings after he left the studio, at a transport café near Trafford Park, which bore the vaguely familiar name Wadi Halfa. It probably had no licence of any kind, and was located in the basement of an otherwise unoccupied building that looked as if it might fall down at any moment. During the three years I spent in Manchester, I sought out Ferber at least once a week at that curious hostelry, and was soon as indifferent as he was to the appalling dishes, a hybrid of the English and the African, that were prepared by the Wadi Halfa's cook, with an incomparable stylish apathy, in a set-up behind the counter that resembled a field kitchen. With a single, sweeping, seemingly slow-motion movement of his left hand (his right was always in his trouser pocket) the cook could take two or three eggs from the box, break them into the pan, and dispose of the shells in the bin. Ferber told me that this cook, who was almost two metres tall, had once been a Maasai chieftain. Now close to eighty, he had travelled (said Ferber), by which highways and byways he could not say, from the south of Kenya to the north of England, in the postwar years. There he soon learnt the rudiments of local cooking, and, giving up the nomadic life, had settled in to his present trade. As for the waiters, noticeably more numerous than the customers, who stood or sat around at the Wadi Halfa wearing expressions of the utmost boredom, Ferber assured me that they were without exception the chieftain's sons, the eldest probably somewhat over sixty, the youngest twelve or thirteen. Since they were each as slim and tall as the other, and all displayed the same disdain in their fine, even features, they were scarcely distinguishable, especially as they would take over from each other at irregular intervals, so that the team of waiters currently on duty was continuously changing. Nonetheless, Ferber, who had observed them closely and used the differences in their ages as an aid to identification, was of the opinion that there were neither more nor less than a dozen waiters, all told, whereas I for my part could never manage to picture those not present at any given moment. It is also worth mentioning that I never once saw any women at the Wadi Halfa, neither family or companions of the boss or his sons nor indeed customers, the clientèle being chiefly workmen from the demolition companies then busy throughout Trafford Park, lorry divers, refuse collectors and others who happened to be out and about.

At every hour of the day and night, the Wadi Halfa was lit by flickering, glaringly bright neon light that permitted not the slightest shadow. When I think back to our meetings in Trafford Park, it is invariably in that unremitting light that I see Ferber, always sitting in the same place in front of a fresco painted by an unknown hand that showed a caravan moving forward from the remotest depths of the picture, across a wavy ridge of dunes, straight towards the beholder. The painter lacked the necessary skill, and the perspective he had chosen was a difficult one, as a result of which both the human figures and the beasts of burden were slightly distorted, so that, if you half shut your eyes, the scene looked like a mirage, quivering in the heat and light. And especially on days when Ferber had been working in charcoal, and the fine powdery dust had given his skin a metallic sheen, he seemed to have just emerged from the desert scene, or to belong in it. He himself once remarked, studying the gleam of graphite on the back of his hands, that in his dreams, both waking and by night, he had already crossed all the earth's deserts of sand and stone. But anyway, he went on, avoiding any further explanation, the darkening of his skin reminded him of an article he had recently read in the paper about silver poisoning, the symptoms of which were not uncommon among professional photographers. According to the article, the British Medical Association's archives contained the description of an extreme case of silver poisoning: in the 1930s there was a photographic lab assistant in Manchester whose body had absorbed so much silver in the course of a lengthy professional life that he had become a kind of photographic plate, which was apparent in the fact (as Ferber solemnly informed me) that the man's face and hands turned blue in strong light, or, as one might say, developed.

One summer evening in 1966, nine or ten months after my arrival in Manchester, Ferber and I were walking along the Ship Canal embankment, past the suburbs of Eccles, Patricroft and Barton upon Irwell on the other side of the black water, towards the setting sun and the scattered outskirts where occasional views opened up, affording an intimation of the marshes that extended there as late as the mid nineteenth century. The Manchester Ship Canal, Ferber told me, was begun in 1887 and completed in 1894. The work was mainly done by a continuously reinforced army of Irish navvies, who shifted some sixty million cubic metres of earth in that period and built the gigantic locks that would make it possible to raise or lower ocean-going steamers up to 150 metres long by five or six metres. Manchester was then the industrial Jerusalem, said Ferber, its entrepreneurial spirit and progressive vigour the envy of the world, and the completion of the immense canal project had made it the largest inland port on earth. Ships of the Canada & Newfoundland Steamship Company, the China Mutual Line, the Manchester Bombay General Navigation Company, and many other shipping lines, plied the docks near the city centre. The loading and unloading never stopped: wheat, nitre, construction timber, cotton, rubber, jute, train oil, tobacco, tea, coffee, cane sugar, exotic fruits, copper and iron ore, steel, machinery, marble and mahogany – everything, in fact, that could possibly be needed, processed or made in a manufacturing metropolis of that order. Manchester's shipping traffic peaked around 1930 and then went into an irreversible decline, till it came to a complete standstill in the late Fifties. Given the motionlessness and deathly silence that lay upon the canal now, it was difficult to imagine, said Ferber, as we gazed back at the city sinking into the twilight, that he himself, in the postwar years, had seen the most enormous freighters on this water. They would slip slowly by, and as they approached the port they passed amidst houses, looming high above the black slate roofs. And in winter, said Ferber, if a ship suddenly appeared out of the mist when one least expected it, passed by soundlessly, and vanished once more in the white air, then for me, every time, it was an utterly incomprehensible spectacle which moved me deeply.

I no longer remember how Ferber came to tell me the extremely cursory version of his life that he gave me at that time, though I do remember that he was loath to answer the questions I put to him about his story and his early years. It was in the autumn of 1943, at the age of eighteen, that Ferber, then a student of art, first went to Manchester. Within months, in early 1944, he was called up. The only point of note concerning that first brief stay in Manchester, said Ferber, was the fact that he had lodged at 104, Palatine Road – the selfsame house where Ludwig Wittgenstein, then a twenty-year-old engineering student, had lived in 1908. Doubtless any retrospective connection with Wittgenstein was purely illusory, but it meant no less to him on that account, said Ferber. Indeed, he sometimes felt as if he were tightening his ties to those who had gone before; and for that reason, whenever he pictured the young Wittgenstein bent over the design of a variable combustion chamber, or test-flying a kite of his own construction on the Derbyshire moors, he was aware of a sense of brotherhood that reached far back beyond his own lifetime or even the years immediately before it. Continuing with his account, Ferber told me that after basic training at Catterick, in a God-forsaken part of north Yorkshire, he volunteered for a paratroop regiment, hoping that that way he would still see action before the end of the war, which was clearly not far off. Instead, he fell ill with jaundice, and was transferred to the convalescent home in the Palace Hotel at Buxton, and so his hopes were dashed. Ferber was compelled to spend more than six months at the idyllic Derbyshire spa town, recovering his health and consumed with rage, as he observed without explanation. It had been a terribly bad time for him, a time scarcely to be endured, a time he could not bear to say any more about. At all events, in early May 1945, with his discharge papers in

his pocket, he had walked the roughly forty kilometres to Manchester to resume his art studies there. He could still see, with absolute clarity, his descent from the fringes of the moorlands after his walk amidst the spring sunshine and showers. From a last bluff he had had a bird's eye view of the city spread out before him, the city where he was to live ever after. Contained by hills on three sides, it lay there as if in the heart of a natural amphitheatre. Over the flatland to the west, a curiously shaped cloud extended to the horizon, and the last rays of sunlight were blazing past its edges, and for a while lit up the entire panorama as if by firelight or Bengal flares. Not until this illumination died (said Ferber) did his eye roam, taking in the crammed and interlinked rows of houses, the textile mills and dying works, the gasometers, chemicals plants and factories of every kind, as far as what he took to be the centre of the city, where all seemed one solid mass of utter blackness, bereft of any further distinguishing features. The most impressive thing, of course, said Ferber, were all the chimneys that towered above the plain and the flat maze of

housing, as far as the eye could see. Almost every one of those chimneys, he said, has now been demolished or taken out of use. But at that time there were still thousands of them, side by side, belching out smoke by day and night. Those square and circular smokestacks, and the countless chimneys from which a yellowy-grey smoke rose, made a deeper impression on me when I arrived than anything else I had previously seen, said Ferber. I can no longer say exactly what thoughts the sight of Manchester prompted in me then, but I believe I felt I had found my destiny. And I also remember, he said, that when at last I was ready to go on I looked down once more over the pale green parklands deep down below, and, half an hour after sunset, saw a shadow, like the shadow of a cloud, flit across the fields – a herd of deer headed for the night.

As I expected, I have remained in Manchester to this day, Ferber continued. It is now twenty-two years since I arrived, he said, and with every year that passes a change of place seems less conceivable. Manchester has taken possession of me for good. I cannot leave, I do not want to leave, I must not. Even the visits I have to make to London once or twice a year oppress and upset me. Waiting at stations, the announcements on the public address, sitting in the train, the country passing by (which is still quite unknown to me), the looks of fellow passengers – all of it is torture to me. That is why I have rarely been anywhere in my life, except of course Manchester; and even here I often don't leave the house or workshop for weeks on end. Only once have I travelled abroad since my youth, two years ago, when I went to Colmar in the summer, and from Colmar via Basle to Lake Geneva. For a very long time I had wanted to see Grünewald's

Isenheim paintings, which were often in my mind as I worked, and especially the "Entombment of Christ", but I never managed to master my fear of travelling. So I was all the more amazed, once I had taken the plunge, to find how easily it went. Looking back from the ferry at the white cliffs of Dover, I even imagined I should be liberated from that moment; and the train ride across France, which I had been particularly afraid of, also went very well. It was a fine day, I had a whole compartment, indeed the entire carriage to myself, the air rushed in at the window, and I felt a kind of festive good spirits rising within me. About ten or eleven in the evening I arrived in Colmar, where I spent a good night at the Hotel Terminus Bristol on the Place de la Gare and the next morning, without delay, went to the museum to look at the Grünewald paintings. The extreme vision of that strange man, which was lodged in every detail, distorted every limb, and infected the colours like an illness, was one I had always felt in tune with, and now I found my feeling confirmed by the direct encounter. The monstrosity of that suffering, which, emanating from the figures depicted, spread to cover the whole of Nature, only to flood back from the lifeless landscape to the humans marked by death, rose and ebbed within me like a tide. Looking at those gashed bodies, and at the witnesses of the execution, doubled up by grief like snapped reeds, I gradually understood that, beyond a certain point, pain blots out the one thing that is essential to its being experienced – consciousness – and so perhaps extinguishes itself; we know very little about this. What is certain, though, is that mental suffering is effectively without end. One may think one has reached the very limit, but there are always more torments to come. One plunges from one abyss into the next. When I was in Colmar, said Ferber, I beheld all of this in precise detail, how one thing had led to another and how it had been afterwards. The flood of memory, little of which remains with me now, began with my recalling a Friday morning some years ago when I was suddenly struck by the paroxysm of pain that a slipped disc can occasion, pain of a kind I had never experienced before. I had simply bent down to the cat, and as I straightened up the tissue tore and the *nucleus pulposus* jammed into the nerves. At least, that is how the doctor later described it. At that moment, all I knew was that I mustn't move even a fraction of an inch, that my whole life had shrunk to that one tiny point of absolute pain, and that even breathing in made everything go black. Until the evening I was rooted in one place in a semi-erect position. How I managed the few steps to the wall, after darkness had fallen, and how I pulled the tartan blanket that was hanging

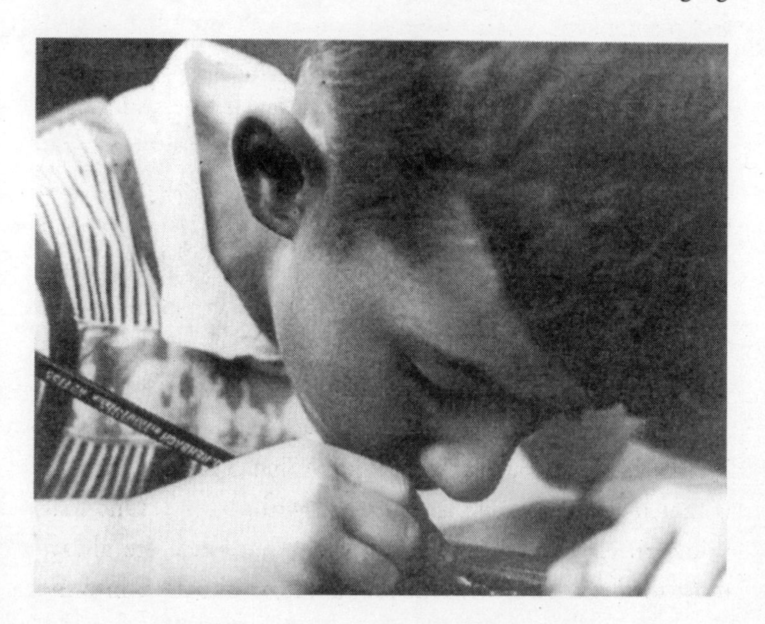

on the back of the chair over my shoulders, I no longer remember. All I now recall is that I stood at that wall all night long with my forehead against the damp, musty plaster, that it grew colder and colder, that the tears ran down my face, that I began to mutter nonsense, and that through it all I felt that being utterly crippled by pain in this way was related, in the most precise manner conceivable, to the inner constitution I had acquired over the years. I also remember that the crooked position I was forced to stand in reminded me, even in my pain, of a photograph my father had taken of me in the second form at school, bent over my writing. In Colmar, at any rate, said Ferber after a lengthy pause, I began to remember, and it was probably those recollections that prompted me to go on to Lake Geneva after eight days, to retrace another old memory that had long been buried and which I had never dared disturb. My father, said Ferber, beginning anew, was an art dealer, and in the summer months he regularly put on what he called special exhibitions in the lobbies of famous hotels. In 1936 he took me with him to one of these exhibitions at the Victoria Jungfrau in Interlaken and then to the Palace at Montreux. Father's shows usually consisted of about five dozen salon pieces in the Dutch manner, in gold frames, or Mediterranean genre scenes in the style of Murillo, and deserted German landscapes – of these, I remember a composition that showed a gloomy heath with two juniper trees, at a distance from each other, in the blood-red glow of the setting sun. As well as I could, at the age of twelve, I helped Father with the hanging, labelling and despatch of these exhibition pieces, which he described as artistic merchandise. By way of a reward for my efforts, Father, who loved the Alps passionately, took me up the

Jungfraujoch in the mountain railway, and from there he showed me the largest glacier in Europe, gleaming snow-white in the midst of summer. The day after the exhibition at the Palace closed, we drove out of Montreux in a hired car, some way along the Rhône valley, and presently turned off to the right, up a narrow and twisting road to a village with a name that struck me as distinctly odd, Miex. From Miex it was a three-hour walk, past the Lac de Tanay, to the summit of Grammont. All the noontide of that blue-skied day in August I lay beside Father on the mountaintop, gazing down into the even deeper blue of the lake, at the country across the lake, over to the faint silhouette of the Jura range, at the bright towns on the far bank, and at St Gingolph, immediately below us but barely visible in a shaft of shadow perhaps fifteen hundred metres deep. On my train journey through Switzerland, which truly is amazingly beautiful, I was already remembering these scenes and images of thirty years before, said Ferber; but they were also strangely threatening, as I saw with increasing clarity during my stay at the Palace, so that in the end I locked the door of my room, pulled down the blinds, and lay in bed for hours at a stretch, which only worsened my incipient anxiety. After about a week it somehow occurred to me that only the reality outside could save me. But instead of strolling around Montreux, or going over to Lausanne, I set off to climb Grammont a second time, regardless of my condition, which by now was quite frail. The day was as bright as it had been the first time, and when I had reached the top, utterly exhausted, there below me was the country around Lake Geneva once again, seemingly completely unchanged, and with no trace of movement but for the one or two tiny boats that left their white wakes on the deep blue water as they proceeded, unbelievably slowly, and the trains that went to and fro at intervals on the far bank. That world, at once near and unattainably far, said Ferber, exerted so powerful an attraction on him that he was afraid he might leap down into it, and might really have done so had not a man of about sixty suddenly appeared before him – like someone who's popped out of the bloody ground. He was carrying a large white gauze butterfly net and said, in an English voice that was refined but quite unplaceable, that it was time to be thinking of going down if one were to be in Montreux for dinner. He had no recollection of having made the descent with the butterfly man, though, said Ferber; in fact the descent had disappeared entirely from his memory, as had his final days at the Palace and the return journey to England. Why exactly this lagoon of oblivion had spread in him, and how far it extended, had remained a mystery to him however hard he thought about it. If he tried to think back to the time in question, he could not see himself again till he was back in the studio, working at a painting which took him almost a full year, with minor interruptions – the faceless portrait "Man with a Butterfly Net". This he considered one of his most unsatisfactory works, because in his view it conveyed not even the remotest impression of the strangeness of the apparition it referred to. Work on the picture of the butterfly man had taken more out of him than any previous painting, for when he started on it, after countless preliminary studies, he not only overlaid it time and again but also, whenever the canvas could no longer withstand the continual scratching-off and re-application of paint, he destroyed it and burnt it several times. The despair at his lack of ability which already tormented him quite enough during the day now invaded his increasingly sleepless nights, so that soon he wept with exhaustion as he worked. In the end he had no alternative but powerful sedatives, which in turn gave him the most horrific hallucinations, not unlike those suffered by St Anthony on the temptation panel of the Isenheim altar-piece. Thus, for instance, he once saw his cat leap vertically into the air and do a backward somersault, whereupon it lay where it fell, rigid. He clearly remembered placing the dead cat in a shoebox and burying it under the almond tree in the yard. Just as clearly, though, there was the cat at its bowl the next morning, looking up at him as if nothing had happened. And once, said Ferber in conclusion, he dreamt (he could not say whether by day or by night) that in 1887 he had opened the great art exhibition in the purpose-built Trafford Park, together with Queen Victoria. Thousands of people were present as, hand in hand with the fat Queen, who gave off an unsavoury odour, he walked through the endless halls

containing 16,000 gold-framed works of art. Almost without exception, said Ferber, the works were items from his father's holdings. In amongst them, however, there were one or two of my own paintings, though to my dismay they differed not at all, or only insignificantly, from the salon pieces. At length, continued Ferber, we passed through a painted *trompe-l'oeil* door (done with astounding skill, as the Queen remarked to me) into a gallery covered in layers of dust, in the greatest possible contrast to the glittering crystal palace, where clearly no one had set foot for years and which, after some hesitation, I recognized as my parents' drawing room. Somewhat to one side, a stranger was sitting on the ottoman. In his lap he was holding a model of the Temple of Solomon, made of pinewood, papier-mâché and gold paint. Frohmann, from Drohobycz, he said, bowing slightly, going on to explain that it had taken him seven years to build the temple, from the biblical description, and that he was now travelling from ghetto to ghetto exhibiting the model. Just look, said Frohmann: you can see every crenellation on the towers, every curtain, every threshold, every sacred vessel. And I, said Ferber, bent down over the diminutive temple and realized, for the first time in my life, what a true work of art looks like.

I had been in Manchester for the best part of three years when, having completed my research, I left the city in the summer of 1969 to follow a plan I had long had of becoming a schoolteacher in Switzerland. On my return from a soot-blackened city that was drifting steadily towards ruin, I was deeply moved by the beauty and variety of the Swiss country-side, which by then had almost slipped my memory, and the sight of the snowy mountains in the distance, the high-lying forests, the autumn light, the frozen watercourses and fields, and the fruit trees in blossom in the meadows, touched my heart more powerfully than I could have anticipated; but nevertheless, for various reasons partly to do with the Swiss attitude to life and partly to do with my position as a teacher, I did not care to stay in Switzerland for long. A bare year had passed when I decided to return to England and to take up the offer of a post I found attractive from several points of view, in Norfolk, which was then considered off the beaten track. If I had still occasionally thought of Ferber and Manchester during my months in Switzerland, my memories faded steadily in the period in England which followed and which, as I sometimes note with amazement, has continued up to the present. Of course Ferber did come to my mind at various times over the long years, but I never succeeded in picturing him properly. His face had become a mere shadow. I assumed that Ferber had been drowned in his labours, but avoided making any closer enquiries. It was not until late November 1989, when by sheer chance I came across a painting bearing his signature in the Tate Gallery (I had gone to see Delvaux's "Sleeping Venus"), that Ferber came alive again in my mind. The painting, about one and a half by two metres, bore a title which struck me as both significant and improbable: "G.I. on her Blue Candlewick Cover". Not long after, I came across Ferber in a Sunday colour supplement, again pretty much by chance, since I have long avoided reading the Sunday papers and especially the magazines that come with them. According to the article, his work now fetched the highest prices on the art market, but Ferber himself, ignoring this development, still lived as he had always done, and continued to work at the easel ten hours a day in his studio near the Manchester docks. For weeks I carried the magazine around with me, glancing time and again at the article, which, I sensed, had unlocked in me a sort of gaol or oubliette. I studied Ferber's dark eye, looking sideways out of a photograph that accompanied the text, and tried, at least with hindsight, to understand what inhibitions or wariness there had been on his part that had kept our conversations away from his origins, despite the fact that such a talk, as I now realized, would have been the obvious thing. In May 1939, at the age of fifteen, Friedrich Maximilian Ferber (so the rather meagre magazine account informed me) left Munich, where his father was an art dealer, for England. The article went on to say that Ferber's parents, who delayed their own departure from Germany for a number of reasons, were taken from Munich to Riga in November 1941, in one of the first deportation trains, and were subsequently murdered there. As I now thought back, it seemed unforgivable that I should have omitted, or failed, in those Manchester times, to ask Ferber the questions he must surely have expected from me; and so, for the first time in a very long while, I went to Manchester once again, a six-hour train journey that criss-crossed the country, through the pine forests and heathlands near Thetford, across the broad lowlands around the Isle of Ely, black at wintertime, past towns and cities each as ugly as the next – March, Peterborough, Loughborough, Nottingham, Alfreton, Sheffield – and past disused industrial plants, slag heaps, belching cooling towers, hills with never a soul about, sheep pastures, stone walls, and on through snow showers, rain, and the ever-changing colours of the sky. By early afternoon I was in Manchester, and immediately set off westwards, through the city, in the direction of the docks. To my surprise,

I had no difficulty in finding my way, since everything in Manchester had essentially remained the same as it had been almost a quarter of a century before. The buildings that had been put up to stave off the general decline were now themselves in the grip of decay, and even the so-called development zones, created in recent years on the fringes of the city centre and along the Ship Canal, to revive the entrepreneurial spirit that so much was being made of, already looked semi-abandoned. The wasteland and the white clouds drifting in from the Irish Sea were reflected in the glinting glass fronts of office blocks, some of which were only half occupied, and some of which were still under construction. Once I was out at the docks it did not take me long to find Ferber's studio. The cobbled yard was unaltered. The almond tree was about to blossom, and when I crossed the threshold it was as if I had been there only yesterday. The same dull light was entering by the window, and the easel still stood in the middle of the room on the black encrusted floor, a black piece of card on it, overworked to the point of being unrecognizable. To judge by the picture clipped to a second easel, the model that had served Ferber for this exercise in destruction was a Courbet

that I had always been especially fond of, "The Oak of Vercingetorix". But Ferber himself, whom I had not noticed at first as I came in from outside, was sitting towards the rear in his red velvet armchair, a cup of tea in his hand, watching his visitor out of the corner of his eye. I was now getting on for fifty, as he had been then, while Ferber himself was almost seventy. By way of welcome he said: Aren't we all getting on! He said it with a throwaway smile, and then, not seeming to me to have aged in the slightest, gestured towards a copy of Rembrandt's portrait of a man with a magnifying glass, which still hung in the same place on the wall as it had twenty-five years before, and added: Only he doesn't seem to get any older.

Following this late reunion, which neither of us had expected, we talked for three whole days far into the night, and a great many more things were said than I shall be able to write down here: concerning our exile in England, the immigrant city of Manchester and its irreversible decline, the Wadi Halfa (which had long ceased to exist), the flugelhorn player Gracie Irlam, my year as a schoolteacher in Switzerland, and my subsequent attempt, also aborted, to settle in Munich, in a German cultural institute. Ferber commented that, purely in terms of time, I was now as far removed from Germany as he had been in 1966; but time, he went on, is an unreliable way of gauging these things, indeed it is nothing but a disquiet of the soul. There is neither a past nor a future. At least, not for me. The fragmentary scenes that haunt my memories are obsessive in character. When I think of Germany, it feels as if there were some kind of insanity lodged in my head. Probably the reason why I have never been to Germany again is that I am afraid to find that this insanity really exists. To me, you see, Germany is a country frozen in the past, destroyed, a curiously extraterritorial place, inhabited by people whose faces are both lovely and dreadful. All of them are dressed in the style of the Thirties, or even earlier fashions, and wearing headgear that does not go with their clothing at all – pilots' helmets, peaked caps, top hats, ear muffs, crossover headbands, and hand-knitted woollen caps. Almost every day a beautiful woman wearing a ball gown made of grey parachute silk and a broad-brimmed hat trimmed with grey roses visits me. Hardly have I sat down in my armchair, tired from work, but I hear her steps outside on the pavement. She sweeps in at the gate, past the almond tree, and there she is, on the threshold of my workshop. Hastily she comes over to me, like a doctor afraid that she may be too late to save a sinking patient. She takes off her hat and her hair tumbles about her shoulders, she strips off her fencing gloves and tosses them onto this little table, and she bends down towards me. I close my eyes in a swoon – and how it goes on after that point, I do not know. One thing is certain: we never say a word. The scene is always a silent one. I think the grey lady understands only her mother tongue, German, which I have not once spoken since I parted from my parents at Oberwiesenfeld airport in Munich in 1939, and which survives in me as no more than an echo, a muted and incomprehensible murmur. It may possibly have something to do with this loss of language, this oblivion, Ferber went on, that my memories reach no further back than my ninth or eighth year, and that I recall little of the Munich years after 1933 other than processions, marches and parades. There seems always to have been a reason for them: May Day or Corpus Christi, carnival or the tenth anniversary of the Putsch, Reichsbauerntag or the inauguration of the Haus der Kunst. They were forever bearing either the Sacred Heart through the city centre or what they called the *Blutfahne*, the banner of blood. On one occasion, said Ferber, they put up trapeziform pedestals draped in chestnut-coloured cloth on either side of the Ludwigstrasse, all the way from the Feldherrnhalle into the heart of Schwabing, and on every one of the pedestals a flame was burning in a shallow iron bowl. At these constant assemblies and parades, the number of different uniforms and insignia noticeably increased. It was as if a new species of humanity, one after another, was evolving before our very eyes. I was filled with wonderment, anger, yearning and revulsion in equal measure; as a child, and then as a teenager, I would stand silently amidst the cheering or awe-struck crowds, ashamed that I did not belong. At home, my parents never talked about the new order in my presence, or only did so obliquely. We all tried desperately to maintain an appearance of normality, even after Father had to hand over the management of his gallery across from the Haus der Kunst, which had opened only the year before, to an Aryan partner. I still did my homework under Mother's supervision; we still went to Schliersee for the skiing in winter, and to Oberstdorf or the Walsertal for our summer holidays; and of those things we could not speak of we simply said nothing. Thus, for instance, all my family and relatives remained largely silent about the reasons why my grandmother Lily Lanzberg took her own life; somehow they seem to have agreed that towards the end she was no longer quite in her right mind. Uncle Leo, Mother's twin brother, with whom we drove from Bad Kissingen to Würzburg after the funeral, at the end of July 1936, was the only one I occasionally heard talk outspokenly about the situation; but this was generally met with disapproval. I now remember (said Ferber) that Uncle Leo, who taught Latin and Greek at a grammar school in Würzburg until he was dismissed, once showed Father a newspaper clipping dating from 1933, with a photograph of the book burning on the Residenzplatz in Würzburg. That photograph, said Uncle, was a forgery. The burning of the books took place on the evening of the 10th of May, he said – he repeated it several times – the books were burnt on the evening of the 10th of May, but since it was already dark, and they couldn't take any decent photographs, they simply took a picture of some other gathering outside the palace, Uncle claimed, and added a swathe of smoke and a dark night sky. In other words, the photographic document published in the paper was a fake. And just as that document was a fake, said Uncle, as if his discovery were the one vital proof, so too everything else has been a fake, from the very start. But Father shook his head without saying a word, either because he was appalled or because he could not assent to Uncle Leo's sweeping verdict. At first I too found the Würzburg story, which Ferber said he was only then remembering for the first time, somewhat on the improbable side; but in the meantime I have tracked down the photograph in question in a Würzburg archive, and as one can easily see there is indeed no doubt that Ferber's

uncle's suspicions were justified. Continuing his account of his visit to Würzburg in summer 1936, Ferber said that one day when they were strolling in the palace gardens Uncle Leo told him that he had been compulsorily retired on the 31st of December the year before and that, in consequence, he was preparing to emigrate from Germany, and was planning to go to England or America shortly. Afterwards we were in the great hall of the palace, and I stood beside Uncle, craning up at Tiepolo's glorious ceiling fresco above the stairwell, which at that time meant nothing to me; beneath the loftiest of skies, the creatures and people of the four realms of the world are assembled on it in fantastic array. Strangely enough, said Ferber, I only thought of that afternoon in Würzburg with Uncle Leo a few months ago, when I was looking through a new book on Tiepolo. For a long time I couldn't tear myself away from the reproductions of the great Würzburg fresco, its light-skinned and dark-skinned beauties, the kneeling Moor with the sunshade and the magnificent Amazon with the feathered headdress. For a whole evening, said Ferber, I sat looking at those pictures with a magnifying glass, trying to see further and further into them. And little by little that summer day in Würzburg came back to me, and the return to Munich, where the general situation and the atmosphere at home were steadily becoming more unbearable, and the silence was thickening. Father, said Ferber, was something of a born comedian or play-actor. He enjoyed life, or rather, he would have enjoyed it; he would have liked to go to the Theater am Gärtnerplatz still, to the revues and wine bars; but, because of the circumstances, the depressive traits that were also in his character overlaid his essentially cheerful nature towards the end of the Thirties. He began to display an absent-mindedness and irritability which I had not seen in him before; both he and Mother put it down to a passing nervousness, which for days at a time would dictate his behaviour. He went to the cinema more and more often, to see cowboy films and the mountaineering films of Luis Trenker. Not once was there any talk of leaving Germany, at least not in my presence, not even after the Nazis had confiscated pictures, furniture and valuables from our home, on the grounds that we had no right to the German heritage. All I remember is that my parents were particularly affronted by the uncouth manner in which the lower ranks stuffed their pockets full of cigarettes and cigarillos. After the Kristallnacht, Father was interned in Dachau. Six weeks later he came home, distinctly thinner and with his hair cropped

short. To me he said not a word about what he had seen and experienced. How much he told Mother, I do not know. Once more, in early 1939, we went to Lenggries for the skiing. It was my last time and I think it was Father's, too. I took a photo of him up on the Brauneck. It is one of the few that have survived from those years, said Ferber. Not long after our trip to Lenggries, Father managed to get a visa for me by bribing the English consul. Mother was counting on their both following me soon. Father was finally determined to leave the country, she said. They only had to make the necessary arrangements. So my things were packed, and on the 17th of May, Mother's fiftieth birthday, my parents took me to the airport. It was a fine, bright morning, and we drove from our house in Sternwartstrasse in Bogenhausen across the Isar, through the Englischer Garten along Tivolistrasse, across the Eisbach, which I still see as clearly as I did then, to Schwabing and then out of the city along Leopoldstrasse towards Oberwiesenfeld. The drive seemed endless to me, said Ferber, probably because none of us said a word. When I asked if he remembered saying goodbye to his parents at the airport, Ferber replied, after a long hesitation, that when he thought back to that May morning at Oberwiesenfeld he could not see his parents. He no longer knew what the last thing his mother or father had said to him was, or he to them, or whether he and his parents had embraced or not. He could still see his parents sitting in the back of the hired car on the drive out to Oberwiesenfeld, but he could not see them at the airport itself. And yet he could picture Oberwiesenfeld down to the last detail, and all these years had been able to envisualize it with that fearful precision, time and time again. The bright concrete strip in front of the open hangar and the deep dark inside it, the swastikas on the rudders of the aircraft, the fenced-off area where he had to wait with the other passengers, the privet hedge around the fence, the groundsman with his wheelbarrow, shovel and brush, the weather station boxes, which reminded him of bee-hives, the cannon at the airfield perimeter – he could see it all with painful clarity, and he could see himself walking across the short grass towards the white Lufthansa Junkers 52, which bore the name Kurt Wüsthoff and the number D–3051. I see myself mounting the wheeled wooden steps, said Ferber, and sitting down in the plane beside a woman in a blue Tyrolean hat, and I see myself looking out of the little square window as we raced across the big, green, deserted airfield, at a distant flock of sheep and the tiny figure of a shepherd. And then I see Munich slowly tilting away below me.

The flight in the Ju52 took me only as far as Frankfurt, said Ferber, where I had to wait for several hours and clear customs. There, at Frankfurt am Main airport, my opened suitcase sat on an ink-stained table while a customs official, without touching a thing, stared into it for a very long time, as if the clothes which my mother had folded and packed in her distinctive, highly orderly way, the neatly ironed shirts or my Norwegian skiing jersey, might possess some mysterious significance. What I myself thought as I looked at my open suitcase, I no longer know; but now, when I think back, it feels as if I ought never to have unpacked it, said Ferber, covering his face with his hands. The BEA plane in which I flew on to London at about three that afternoon, he continued, was a Lockheed Electra. It was a fine flight. I saw Belgium from the air, the Ardennes, Brussels, the straight roads of Flanders, the sand dunes of Ostende, the coast, the white cliffs of Dover, the green hedgerows and hills south of London, and then, appearing on the horizon like a low grey range of hills, the island capital itself. We landed at half past five at Hendon airfield. Uncle Leo met me. We drove into the city, past endless rows of suburban houses so indistinguishable from one another that I found them depressing yet at the same time vaguely ridiculous. Uncle was living in a little émigré hotel in Bloomsbury, near the British Museum. My first night in England was spent in that hotel, on a peculiar, high-framed bed, and was sleepless not so much because of my distress as because of the way that one is pinned down, in English beds of that kind, by bedding which has been tucked under the mattress all the way round. So the next morning, the 18th of May, I was bleary-eyed and weary when I tried on my new school uniform at Baker's in Kensington, with my uncle – a pair of short black trousers, royal blue knee-length socks, a blazer of the same colour, an orange shirt, a striped tie, and a tiny cap that would not stay put on my full shock of hair no matter how I tried. Uncle, given the funds at his disposal, had found me a third-rate public school at Margate, and I believe that when he saw me kitted out like that he was as close to tears as I was when I saw myself in the mirror. And if the uniform felt like a fool's motley, expressly designed to heap scorn upon me, then the school itself, when we arrived there that afternoon, seemed like a prison or mental asylum. The circular bed of dwarf conifers in the curve of the drive, the grim façade capped by battlements of sorts, the rusty bell-pull beside the open door, the school janitor who came limping out of the darkness of the hall, the colossal oak stairwell, the coldness of all the rooms, the smell of coal, the incessant cooing of the decrepit pigeons that perched everywhere on the roof, and numerous other sinister details I no longer remember, conspired to make me think that I would go mad in next to no time in that establishment. It presently emerged, however, that the regime of the school – where I was to spend the next few years – was in fact fairly lax, sometimes to the point of anarchy. The headmaster and founder of the school, a man by the name of Lionel Lynch-Lewis, was a bachelor of almost seventy, invariably dressed in the most eccentric manner and scented with a discreet hint of lilac; and his staff, no less eccentric, more or less left the pupils, who were mainly the sons of minor diplomats from unimportant countries, or the offspring of other itinerants, to their own devices. Lynch-Lewis took the view that nothing was more damaging to the development of young adolescents than a regular school timetable. He maintained that one learnt best and most easily in one's free time. This attractive concept did in fact bear fruit for some of us, but others ran quite disturbingly wild as a result. As for the parrot-like uniform which we had to wear and which, it turned out, had been designed by Lynch-Lewis himself, it formed the greatest possible contrast to the rest of his pedagogical approach. At best, the outré riot of colour we were obliged to wear fitted in with the excessive emphasis placed by Lynch-Lewis on the cultivation of correct English, which in his view could mean only turn-of-the-century stage English. Not for nothing was it rumoured in Margate that our teachers were all, without exception, recruited from the ranks of actors who had failed, for whatever reason, in their chosen profession. Oddly enough, said Ferber, when I look back at my time in Margate I cannot say whether I was happy or unhappy, or indeed what I was. At any rate, the amoral code that governed life at school gave me a certain sense of freedom, such as I had not had till then – and, that being so, it grew steadily harder for me to write my letters home or to read the letters that arrived from home every fortnight. The correspondence became more of a chore, and when the letters stopped coming, in November 1941, I was relieved at first, in a way that now strikes me as quite terrible. Only gradually did it dawn on me that I would never again be able to write home; in fact, to tell the truth, I do not know if I have really grasped it to this day. But it now seems to me that the course of my life, down to the tiniest detail, was ordained not only by the deportation of my parents but also by the delay with which the news of their death reached me, news I could not believe at first and the meaning of which only sank in by degrees. Naturally, I took steps, consciously or unconsciously, to keep at bay thoughts of my parents' sufferings and of my own misfortune, and no doubt I succeeded sometimes in maintaining a certain equability by my self-imposed seclusion; but the fact is that that tragedy in my youth struck such deep roots within me that it later shot up again, put forth evil flowers, and spread the poisonous canopy over me which has kept me so much in the shade and dark in recent years.

In early 1942 (Ferber concluded, the evening before I left Manchester), Uncle Leo embarked at Southampton for New York. Before he left he visited Margate one last time, and we agreed that I would follow him in the summer, when I had completed my last year at school. But when the time came I did not want to be reminded of my origins by anything or anyone, so instead of going to New York, into the care of my uncle, I decided to move to Manchester on my own. Inexperienced as I was, I imagined I could begin a new life in Manchester, from scratch; but instead, Manchester reminded me of everything I was trying to forget. Manchester is an immigrant city, and for a hundred and fifty years, leaving aside the poor Irish, the immigrants were chiefly Germans and Jews, manual workers, tradesmen, freelancers, retailers and wholesalers, watchmakers, hatters, cabinet-makers, umbrella makers, tailors, bookbinders, typesetters, silversmiths, photographers, furriers and glovers, scrap merchants, hawkers, pawnbrokers, auctioneers, jewellers, estate agents, stockbrokers, chemists and doctors. The Sephardic Jews, who had been settled in Manchester for a long time and had names like Besso, Raphael, Cattun, Calderon, Farache, Negriu, Messulam or di Moro, made little distinction between the Germans and other Jews with names like Leibrand, Wohlgemuth, Herzmann, Gottschalk, Adler, Engels, Landeshut, Frank, Zirndorf, Wallerstein, Aronsberg, Haarbleicher, Crailsheimer, Danziger, Lipmann or Lazarus. Throughout the nineteenth century, the German and Jewish influence was stronger in Manchester than in any other European city; and so, although I had intended to move in the opposite direction, when I arrived in Manchester I had come home, in a sense, and with every year I have spent since then in this birthplace of industrialization, amidst the black façades, I have realized more clearly than ever that I am here, as they used to say, to serve under the chimney. Ferber said nothing more. For a long time he stared into space, before sending me on my way with a barely perceptible wave of his left hand. When I returned to the studio the following morning to take my leave of him he handed me a brown paper package tied with string, containing a number of photographs and almost a hundred pages of handwritten memoirs penned by his mother in the Sternwartstrasse house between 1939 and 1941, which showed (said Ferber) that obtaining a visa had become increasingly difficult and that the plans his father had made for their emigration had necessarily grown more complex with every week that passed – and, as his mother had clearly understood, impossible to carry out. Mother wrote not a word about the events of the moment, said Ferber, apart from the odd oblique glance at the hopeless situation she and Father were in; instead, with a passion that was beyond his understanding, she wrote of her childhood in the village of Steinach, in lower Franconia, and her youth in Bad Kissingen. In the time that had passed since they were written, said Ferber, he had read the memories his mother had committed to paper, presumably not least with himself in mind, only twice. The first time, after he received the package, he had skimmed over them. The second time he had read them meticulously, many years later. On that second occasion, the memoirs, which at points were truly wonderful, had seemed to him like one of those evil German fairy tales in which, once you are under the spell, you have to carry on to the finish, till your heart breaks, with whatever work you have begun – in this case, the remembering, writing and reading. That is why I would rather you took this package, Ferber said, and saw me out to the yard, where he walked with me as far as the almond tree.

The manuscript which Ferber gave me on that morning in Manchester is before me now. I shall try to convey in excerpts what the author, whose maiden name was Luisa Lanzberg, recounts of her early life. At the very beginning she writes that not only she and her brother Leo were born at Steinach, near Bad Kissingen, but also her father Lazarus, and her grandfather Löb before him. The family was recorded as living in the village, which had formerly been under the jurisdiction of the prince-bishops of Würzburg and a third of whose inhabitants were Jews long resident there, at least as far back as the late seventeenth century. It almost goes without saying that there are no Jews in Steinach now, and that those who live there have difficulty remembering those who were once their neighbours and whose homes and property they appropriated, if indeed they remember them at all. From Bad Kissingen the road to Steinach goes by way of Grossenbrach, Kleinbrach, and Aschach with its castle and Graf Luxburg's brewery. From there it climbs the steep Aschacher Leite, where Lazarus (Luisa writes) always got down from his calèche so that the horses would not have so hard a job of it. From the top, the road runs down, along the edge of the wood, to Höhn, where the fields open out and the hills of the Rhön can be seen in the distance. The Saale meadows spread before you, the Windheim woods nestle in a gentle curve, and there are the tip of the church tower and the old castle – Steinach! Now the road crosses the stream and enters the village, up to the square by the inn, then down to the right to the lower part of the village, which Luisa calls her real home. That is where the Lions live, she writes, where we get oil for the lamps. There lives Meier Frei, the merchant, whose return from the annual Leipzig trade fair is always a big event. There lives Gessner the baker, to whom we took our Sabbath meal on Friday evenings, Liebmann the slaughterer, and Salomon Stern, the flour merchant. The poorhouse, which usually had no occupants, and the fire station with the slatted shutters on the tower, were in the lower part of the village, and so was the old castle with its cobbled forecourt and the Luxburg arms over the gateway. By way of Federgasse, which (Luisa writes) was always full of geese and which she was afraid to walk down as a child, past Simon Feldhahn's haberdashery and Fröhlich the plumber's house with its green tin shingle cladding, you come to a square shaded by a gigantic chest-nut tree. In the house on the other side – before which the square divides into two roads like waves at the bow of a ship, and behind which the Windheim woods rise – I was born and grew up (so the memoir in front of me reads), and there I lived until my sixteenth year, when, in January 1905, we moved to Kissingen.

Now I am standing in the living room once again, writes Luisa. I have walked through the gloomy, stone-flagged hall, have placed my hand cautiously on the handle, as I do almost every morning at that time, I have pushed it down and opened the door, and inside, standing barefoot on the white scrubbed floorboards, I look around in amazement at all the nice things in the room. There are two green velvet armchairs with knotted fringes all round, and between the windows that face onto the square is a sofa in the same style. The table is of light-coloured cherrywood. On it are a fan-like frame with five photographs of our relatives in Mainstockheim and Leutershausen and, in a frame of its own, a picture of Papa's sister, who people say was the most beautiful girl for miles around, a real Germania. Also on the table is a china swan with its wings spread, and in it, in a white lace frill, our dear Mama's evergreen bridal bouquet, beside the silver menora which is required on Friday evenings and for which Papa cuts paper cuffs especially every time, to prevent the wax dripping from the candles. On the tallboy by the wall, opened at a page, lies a folio-sized volume ornately bound in red with golden tendrils of vine. This, says Mama, is the works of her favourite poet, Heine, who is also the favourite poet of Empress Elisabeth. Next to it is the little basket where the newspaper, the *Münchner Neueste Nachrichten*, is kept, which Mama is immersed in every evening despite the fact that Papa, who goes to bed far earlier, always tells her that is is not healthy to read so late at night. The hoya plant is on the cane table in the bay of the east window. Its leaves are firm and dark, and it has a lot of pink-hearted umbels consisting of white, furry stars. When I come down early in the mornings, the sun is already shining into the room and gleaming on the drops of honey that cling to every little star. I can see through the leaves and flowers into the grassy garden where the hens are out pecking. Franz, our stable boy, a very taciturn albino, will have hitched the horses to the calèche by the time Papa is ready to leave, and over there, across the fence, is a tiny house under an elder, where you can usually see Kathinka Strauss at this time. Kathinka is a spinster of perhaps forty, and people say she is not quite right in the head. When the weather permits, she spends her day walking around the chestnut tree in the square, clockwise or anti-clockwise according to whim, knitting something that she plainly never finishes. Though there is little else that she can call her own, she always wears the most outrageous bonnets on these walks; one, which featured a seagull's wing, I remember particularly well because Herr Bein the teacher referred to it in school, telling us we should never kill any creature merely in order to adorn ourselves with its feathers.

Though Mother is long reluctant to let us out of the home, Leo and I are sent to the day nursery when we are four or five. We do not need to go till after morning prayers. It is all very straightforward. The Sister is already in the yard. You go up to her and say: Frau Adelinde, may I have a ball, please? Then you take the ball across the yard and down the steps to the playground. The playground is at the bottom of the broad moat that circles the old castle, where there are now colourful flower beds and vegetable patches. Right above the playground, in a long suite of rooms in the almost completely deserted castle, lives Regina Zufrass. As everyone knows, she is a terribly busy woman and is always hard at work, even on Sundays. Either she is looking after her poultry or you see her in amongst the beanpoles or she is mending the fence or rummaging in one of the rooms, which are far too big for her and her husband. We even saw Regina Zufrass up on the roof once, fixing the weather vane, and we watched with bated breath, expecting her to fall off at any moment and land on the balcony with every bone in her body broken. Her husband, Jofferle, jobs as a waggoner in the village. Regina is none too pleased with him, and he for his part, so they say, is frightened to go home to her. Often people have to be sent to look for him. They tend to find him drunk, sprawled out beside the overturned hay-cart. The horses have long been used to all this and stay patiently by the up-ended waggon. At length the hay is loaded back on and Jofferle is fetched home by Regina. The next day, the green shutters at their windows remain shut, and when we children are eating our sandwiches down in the playground we wonder what can be going on in there. And then, every Thursday morning Mama draws a fish on the waxed paper she wraps the sandwiches in, so that we won't forget to buy half a dozen barbels from the fish man on our way home from the kindergarten. In the afternoon, Leo and I walk hand in hand along the Saale, on the bank where there is a dense copse of willows and alders, and rushes grow, past the sawmill and across the little bridge, where we stop to look down at the golden ringlets round the pebbles on the riverbed before we go on to the fish man's cottage, which is surrounded by bushes. First we have to wait in the parlour while the fish man's wife fetches the fish man. A fat-bellied white coffeepot with a cobalt blue knob is always on the table, and sometimes it seems as if it fills the whole room. The fish man appears in the doorway and takes us straight out through the slightly sloping garden, past his radiant dahlias, down to the Saale, where he takes out the barbels one by one from a big wooden crate in the water. When we eat them for supper we are not allowed to speak because of the bones, and have to keep as quiet as fish ourselves. I never felt particularly comfortable about those meals, and the skewed fish-eyes often went on watching me even in my sleep.

In summer, on the Sabbath, we often take a long walk to Bad Bocklet, where we can stroll around the colonnaded hall and watch the fashionably dressed people taking coffee; or, if it is too hot for a walk, we sit in the late afternoon with the Liebermanns and the Feldhahns in the shade of the chestnut trees by the bowling alley in Reuss's beer garden. The men have beer and the children have lemonade; the women can never decide what they want, and only take a sip of everything, while they cut up the Sabbath loaves and salted beef. After supper, some of the men play billiards, which is thought very daring and progressive. Ferdinand Lion even smokes a cigar! Afterwards they all go to the synagogue together. The women pack the things up and as dusk falls they make their way home with the children. Once, on his way home, Leo is wretched because of his new sailor's outfit, made of starched bright blue and white cotton – mainly because of the fat tie and the bibbed collar that hangs over his shoulders, sporting crossed anchors which Mother sat up very late embroidering the night before. Not until we are sitting on the front steps, by which time it is already dark, watching the storm clouds shift in the sky, does he gradually forget his misery. Once

Father is home, the candle made of many interwoven strands of wax is lit to mark the end of the Sabbath. We smell the little spice-box and go upstairs to bed. Soon dazzling white lightning is flashing across the sky, and the crashes of thunder set the whole house shaking. We stand at the window. There are moments when it is brighter than daylight outside. Clumps of hay are afloat on the swirling waters in the gutters. Then the storm passes over, but presently returns once more. Papa says it cannot make it over Windheim woods.

On Sunday afternoon Papa does his accounts. He takes a small key out of a leather pouch, unlocks the gleaming walnut bureau, opens the centre section, puts the key back into the pouch, sits down with a certain ceremony, and, settling himself, takes out the hefty account book. For an hour or so he makes entries and notes in this book and a number of smaller ones, and on pieces of paper cut to various sizes; softly moving his lips, he adds up long columns of figures and makes calculations, and, depending on what the results are like, his face will brighten up or cloud over for a time. A great many special things are kept in the numerous drawers of the bureau – deeds, certificates, correspondence, Mama's jewellery, and a broad ribbon to which large and small pieces of silver are attached by narrow braids of silk, as if they were medals or decorations: the *hollegrasch* coins that Leo is given by his godfather Selmar in Leutershausen every year, which I covetously marvel at. Mama sits in the living room with Papa, reading the *Münchner Neueste Nachrichten* – all the things she did not get round to reading during the week, for preference the spa columns and a miscellany feature. Whenever she comes across something incredible or remarkable she reads it out to Papa, who has to stop his adding up for a while. Perhaps because I couldn't get the story of Paulinchen, the girl who went up in flames, out of my head at that time, I can hear Mama even now telling Papa in her very own theatrical way (in her youth she had dreamt of being an actress) that ladies' dresses could now be fireproofed, for an exceedingly low cost, by immersing the material they were to be made from in a solution of zinc chloride. Even the finest of materials, I still hear Mama informing Papa, can be held to a naked flame after it has been thus treated, and it will char to ash without catching fire. If I am not with my parents in the living room on those eternally long Sundays, I am upstairs in the green room. In summer, when it is hot, the windows are open but the shutters are closed, and the light that enters makes a slanted Jacob's ladder pattern in the twilight around me. It is very quiet in the house, and throughout the neighbourhood. In the afternoon, the carriages out on excursions from the spa at Kissingen pass through the village. You can hear the horses' hooves from a long way off. I open one of the shutters a little and look down the road. The coaches drive via Steinach to Neustadt and Neuhaus and on to Salzburg castle, and in them the summer spa clientèle sit facing each other, grand ladies and gentlemen and, not infrequently, real Russian celebrities. The ladies are very finely turned out in feather bonnets and veils and with parasols of lace or brightly coloured silk. The village boys turn cartwheels right in front of the carriages, and the elegant passengers toss them copper coins by way of reward.

Autumn arrives, and the autumn holidays are approaching. First comes Rosh Hashanah, bringing in the New Year. The day before, all the rooms are swept, and on the eve Mama and Papa go to the synagogue, wearing their festive best: Papa in his frock coat and top hat, Mama in her deep blue velvet dress and the bonnet made entirely of white lilac blossom. Meanwhile, at home, Leo and I spread a starched linen cloth on the table and place the wine glasses on it, and under our parents' plates we put our New Year letters, written in our finest hand. A week and a half later is Yom Kippur. Father, in his death robes, moves about the house like a ghost. A mood of rue and penitence prevails. None of us will eat until the stars rise. Then we wish each other *ein gutes Anbeißen.* And four days later it is already the Feast of Tabernacles. Franz has put up the trellis for the sukkah under the elder, and we have decorated it with colourful garlands of glossy paper and long chains of threaded rosehips. From the ceiling hang ruddy-cheeked apples, yellow pears and golden-green grapes which Aunt Elise sends us every year from Mainstockheim in a little box lined with wood-shavings. On the two main and four half feast days we shall take our meals in the sukkah, unless the weather is exceptionally bad and cold. Then we stay in the kitchen, and only Papa will sit out in the bower, eating all by himself – a sign that winter is gradually coming. It is also at this time of the year that a wild boar the Prince Regent has shot in the Rhön is brought to Steinach, where its bristles are singed off outside the smithy on a wood fire. At home we study the May & Edlich catalogue from Leipzig, a thick compendious volume that reveals the entire wondrous world of merchandise, page after page, classified and described. Out of doors the colours gradually fade away. Our winter clothes are fetched out. They smell of naphthalene. Towards the end of November the Young Progressives' Club holds a masked ball at Reuss's. Frau Müntzer from Neustadt has made Mama a dress of raspberry-coloured silk for the occasion. The gown is long and flounced very elegantly at the hem. The children are allowed to watch the opening of the ball from the doorway to the next room. The hall is abuzz with festive murmuring. To set the mood, the band plays tunes from operettas, softly, till Herr Hainbuch, who works for the forestry commission, climbs onto the dais and, by way of an official start to the occasion, delivers a speech in praise of the fatherland. Glasses are raised, a flourish from the band, the masks gaze seriously into each other's eyes, another flourish, and the landlord, Herr Reuss, carries in a black box with a tulip-shaped metal funnel – the new gramophone, which pours forth real music without one's needing to do a thing. We are speechless with wonder. The ladies and gentlemen take their positions for a polonaise. Silberberg, the cobbler, quite unrecognizable in his tails, black tie, tie pin and patent leather shoes, walks ahead, conducting with a baton. Behind him come the couples, wheeling and twirling about the hall in every conceivable kind of way. The loveliest of them all, by far, is Aline Feldhahn as the Queen of the Night, in a dark dress bestrewn with stars. She is partnered by Siegfried Frey, wearing his hussar's uniform. Aline and Siegfried later married and had two children, but Siegfried, who was said to have a taste for dissipation, suddenly disappeared, and neither Aline nor old Löb Frey nor anyone else ever found out what became of him. Kathinka Strauss, though, claimed that Siegfried emigrated, to Argentina or Panama.

We have been going to school for a few years now. It is a school where we are all taught together in one form, exclusively for Jewish children. Our teacher, Salomon Bein, whose excellence the parents miss no opportunity to praise, imposes strict discipline, and sees himself first and foremost as a loyal servant of the state. Together with his lady wife and his unmarried sister Regine, he lives in the schoolhouse. In the mornings, when we cross the yard, he is already there in the doorway, spurring latecomers along by shouting *hopp! hopp!* and clapping his hands. In the classroom, after the blessing – *Thou who hast made the day, O Lord* – and after we have sharpened our slate pencils and cleaned our quill pens, jobs I dislike and which Herr Bein supervises closely, we are delegated to various tasks in rotation. Some are assigned to practise their handwriting; others have to do sums; yet others have to write an essay, or draw in their local history books. One group has visual instruction. A scroll is fetched out from the back of the cupboard and hung in front of the blackboard. The whole picture is of nothing but snow, with one coal-black raven in the middle. During the first one or two periods, especially in winter when the daylight never really brightens, I am always very slow about my work. I look out through the blue panes and see the deaf and dumb daughter of Stern, the flour merchant, on the other side of the yard, sitting at her work bench in her little room. She makes artificial flowers out of wire, crêpe and tissue paper, dozens of them, day in, day out, year in, year out. In nature study we learn about real flowers: larkspur, Turk's cap lily, loosestrife and lady's smock. We also learn about red ants and whales, from the animal kingdom. And once, when the village street is being newly surfaced, the teacher draws a picture on the blackboard, in coloured chalks, of the Vogelsberg as an erupting volcano, and explains where the blocks of basalt come from. He also has a collection of colourful stones in his minerals cabinet – rose quartz, rock crystal, amethyst, topaz and tourmaline. We draw a long line to mark how much time it has taken for them to form. Our entire lives would not even show as the tiniest dot on that line. Even so, the hours at school stretch as vast as the Pacific Ocean, and it takes an eternity till Moses Lion, who is sent to fetch wood almost every day by way of punishment, comes back up from the wood store with a basketful. Then, before we know it, Hanukkah is upon us, and it is Herr Bein's birthday. The day before, we decorate the walls of the classroom with branches of fir and little blue and yellow flags. We place the present on the teacher's desk. I remember that on one occasion it was a red velvet blanket, and once a copper hot-water bottle. On the morning of the birthday we all gather early in the classroom, in our best clothes. Then the teacher arrives, followed by his wife and the slightly dwarfish Fräulein Regine. We all stand up and say: Good morning, Herr Bein! Good morning, Frau Bein! Good morning, Fräulein Regine! Our teacher, who has of course long since known what was being prepared, affects to be completely surprised by his present and the decorations. He raises a hand to his forehead, several times, shaking his head, as if he does not know what to say, and, deeply touched, walks up and down the class, thanking each one of us effusively. There are no lessons today; instead, stories and German legends of old are read aloud. We also have a guessing game. For instance, we have to guess the three things that give and take in infinite plenty. Of course no one knows the answer, which Herr Bein then tells us in tones of great significance: the earth, the sea, and the Reich. Perhaps the best thing about that day is that, before we go home, we are allowed to jump over the Hanukkah candles, which have been fixed to the threshold with drops of wax. It is a long winter. At home, Papa does exercises with us in the evening. The geese are gone from their hutch. Soon after, parts of them are preserved in boiling hot fat. Some village women come to slice the quills from the feathers. They sit in the spare room, each with a heap of down in front of her, slicing almost the whole night long. It looks as if snow has fallen. But the next morning, when we get up, the room is so clean, so devoid of feathers, that you'd think nothing had ever happened. Early in the year, spring cleaning has to be done in preparation for Passover. It is worse at school. Frau Bein and Fräulein Regine are at it for at least a week. The mattresses are taken out to the yard, the bedding is hung over the balcony, the floors are newly waxed, and all the cooking utensils are immersed in boiling water. We children have to sweep the classroom and wash the shutters with soapsuds. At home, too, all the rooms and chests are cleared out. The bustle is dreadful. The evening before Passover, Mama sits down for a while for the first time in days. Meanwhile, Father's job is to go around the house with a goose feather checking to see that not a single crumb of bread is still to be found.

It is autumn again, and Leo is now at grammar school in Münnerstadt, a two-hour walk from Steinach, where he is living at Lindwurm the hatter's. His meals are sent to him twice a week – half a dozen little pots, stacked in a carrier. Lindwurm's daughter only has to warm them up. Inconsolable at having to go to school alone from now on, I fall ill. At least every other day I run a temperature and sometimes I am quite delirious. Dr Homburger prescribes elder juice and cold compresses. My bed has been made up on the sofa in the yellow room. For almost three weeks I lie there. Time and again I count the pieces of soap in the pyramid stacked on the marble top of the washstand, but I never arrive at the same total twice. The little yellow dragons on the wallpaper haunt me even in my dreams. I am often in great turmoil. When I wake up, I see the jars of preserves ranged on the chest and in the cold compartments of the tiled stove. I try in vain to work out what they mean. They don't mean anything, says Mama, they're just cherries, plums and pears. Outside, she tells me, the swallows are already gathering. At night, in my sleep, I can hear the swishing flight of great flocks of migrating birds as they pass over the house. When at last my condition improves somewhat, the windows are opened wide one bright Friday afternoon. From my position on the sofa I can see the whole Saale valley and the road to Höhn, and I can see Papa returning from Kissingen by that road, in the calèche. Just a little later, still wearing his hat on his head, he comes into my room. He has brought me a wooden box of sweets with a peacock butterfly painted on it. That evening, a hundredweight of apples, goldings and red calvilles, are laid down for winter on the floor of the next room. Their scent puts me to a more peaceful sleep than I have known for a long time, and when Dr Homburger examines me the next morning he pronounces me perfectly healthy again. But then, when the summer holidays are starting nine months later, it is Leo's turn. He has a lung complaint, and Mama insists that it comes from his airless lodgings at Lindwurm's, and the lead vapours from the hatter's workshop. Dr Homburger agrees. He prescribes a mixture of milk and Selters water, and orders Leo to spend a lot of time in the healthy air of the Windheim pine forests. Now a basket of sandwiches, curd cheese and boiled eggs is made up every morning. I pour Leo's health drink through a funnel into green bottles. Frieda, our cousin from Jochsberg, goes to the woods with us, as supervisor, as it were. She is already sixteen, very beautiful, and has a very long, thick, blonde plait. In the afternoon, Carl Hainbuch, the chief forester's son, invariably just happens to make an appearance, and walks for hours beneath the trees with Frieda. Leo, who reveres his cousin more than anyone, sits on the very top of one of the erratic boulders, watching the romantic scene with displeasure. What interests me most are the countless glossy black stag beetles in the Windheim woods. I track their crooked wanderings with a patient eye. At times it looks as if something has shocked them, physically, and it seems as if they have fainted. They lie there motionless, and it feels as if the world's heart had stopped. Only when you hold your own breath do they return from death to life, only then does time begin to pass again. Time. What time was all that? How slowly the days passed then! And who was that strange child, walking home, tired, with a tiny blue and white jay's feather in her hand?

If I think back nowadays to our childhood in Steinach (Luisa's memoirs continue at another point), it often seems as if it had been open-ended in time, in every direction – indeed, as if it were still going on, right into these lines I am now writing. But in reality, as I know only too well, childhood ended in January 1905 when the house and fields at Steinach were auctioned off and we moved into a new three-storey house in Kissingen, on the corner of Bibrastrasse and Ehrhardstrasse. Father had bought it one day, without hesitation, from Kiesel the builder, for a price of 66,000 gold marks, a sum which struck us all as the stuff of myth, and most of which he had raised on a mortgage with a Frankfurt bank, a fact which it took Mama a long time to accept. The

Lazarus Lanzberg stables had been doing better and better in recent years, supplying as far afield as the Rhineland, Brandenburg and Holstein, buying everywhere, and leaving all their customers well pleased and satisfied. The contract Papa had won as supplier and provisioner to the army, which he proudly mentioned whenever he had the chance, had doubtless been the decisive factor in giving up farming, moving from backwater Steinach, and finally establishing a position in middle-class life. At that time I was almost sixteen, and believed that a completely new world, even lovelier than that of childhood, would be revealed to me in Kissingen. In some respects that was really how it was, but in others the Kissingen years up until my marriage in 1921 seem in retrospect to have marked the first step on a path that grew narrower day by day and led inevitably to the point I have now arrived at. I find it difficult to think back to my youth in Kissingen. It is as if the gradual dawn of what was called the serious side of life, the minor and major disappointments that soon began to mount up, had affected my ability to take things in. And so there is a good deal I can no longer picture. Even of our arrival in Kissingen I have only fragmentary memories. I know it was bitterly cold, there was endless work to be done, my fingers were frozen, for days the house refused to warm up despite the fact that I poked the coals in the Irish stoves in all the rooms; the hoya plant had not survived the move; and the cats had run away, back to the old home, and, though Papa went back especially to Steinach, they were nowhere to be found. To me the house, which the people of Kissingen soon took to calling the Lanzberg Villa, always remained essentially a strange place. The vast, echoing stairwell; the linoleum flooring in the hall; the corridor at the

back where the telephone hung over the laundry basket and you had to hold the heavy receivers to your ears with both hands; the pale, hissing gaslight; the sombre Flemish furniture with its carved columns – there was something distinctly creepy about all of it, and at times I feel quite definitely that it did steady and irreparable harm to me. Only once, if I remember rightly, did I ever sit on the window seat in the drawing room, which was painted with foliage and tendrils like a festive bower, and from the ceiling of which a brand new brass Sabbath-lamp hung down, also fuelled by gas; I leafed through a page or two of the blue velvet postcard album which had its place on the shelf of the smoking table, and felt like a visitor, passing through. Often in the mornings or evenings, when I looked out of my top floor window across the flower beds of the spa nursery gardens to the green, wooded hills all around, I felt like a maid. From the very first spring we rented out several rooms in the house. Mother, who ran the household, was an exacting teacher of domestic management. At six o'clock, right after I got up, my first task was to give the white chickens in the garden their measure of grain and fetch in the eggs. Then breakfast had to be made, the rooms tidied, the vegetables trimmed, and lunch cooked. In the afternoons, for a while, I did a course in shorthand and book-keeping that was taught by nuns. Frau Ignatia was very proud of me. At other times I took the children of visitors to the spa for walks in the public gardens – for instance, Herr Weintraub's fat little boy. Herr Weintraub was a timber merchant and came every year from Perm in Siberia, because Jews (so he said) were not allowed at watering places in Russia. From about four o'clock I would sit out in the chalet darning or crocheting, and in the evening there was the vegetable patch to be watered, with water from the well – the tap water cost too much, claimed Papa. I could go to evening concerts only if Leo was home from the grammar school.

Usually his friend Armand Wittelsbach, who later became an antiques dealer in Paris, would collect us after dinner. I would wear a white dress and stroll through the park between Armand and Leo. On occasions the spa gardens were illuminated: there would be Chinese lanterns strung across the avenues, shedding colourful, magical light. The fountains in front of the Regent's building would jet silver and gold alternately. But at ten o'clock the spell broke and we had to be home. Part of the way, Armand would walk on his hands beside me. I also remember a birthday outing with Armand and Leo. We set out at five in the morning, first towards Klausenhof and from there through the beech woods, where we picked big bunches of lily of the valley, back to Kissingen. We had been invited to breakfast with the Wittelsbachs. It was about that time, too, that we looked out for Halley's comet at night, and once there was a total eclipse of the sun in the early afternoon. It was dreadful to see the shadow of the moon slowly blotting out the sun, the leaves of the rambling rose on the balcony (where we stood with our soot-darkened pieces of glass) seeming to wither, and the birds flapping about in a frightened panic. And I recall that it was on the day after that Laura Mandel and her father first visited us from Trieste. Herr Mandel was nearly eighty but Laura was just our own age, and both of them made the greatest imaginable impression on me, Herr Mandel on account of his elegant appearance – he wore the most stylish linen suits and broad-brimmed straw hats – and Laura (who only ever called her father Giorgio), because of her firm, freckled forehead and her wonderful eyes, which were often rather misty. During the day, Herr Mandel would usually sit somewhere that was partly in the shade – by the silver poplar in our garden, on a bench in Luitpold Park, or on the terrace of the Wittelsbacher Hof hotel – reading the papers, making occasional notes, and often simply lost in thought. Laura said he had long been busy projecting an empire in which nothing ever happened, for he detested nothing more than enterprises, developments, great events, changes, or incidents of any kind. For her part, Laura was all for revolution. I once went to the theatre in Kissingen with her when some Viennese operetta – I no longer know if it was the *Zigeunerbaron* or *Rastlbinder* – was being performed to mark the Austrian Emperor Franz Josef's birthday. First the orchestra played the Austrian national anthem. Everyone stood up except Laura, who remained demonstratively seated because – coming from Trieste – she could not stand Austrians. What she said concerning this was the first political thought I ever came across in my life, and how often have I not wished, of late, that Laura were here again to discuss things with me. For several years she stayed with us during the summer months, the last time being that especially lovely season when both of us turned twenty-one, myself on the 17th of May and she on the 7th of July. I remember her birthday particularly. We had taken the little steamer upriver to the salt-vapour frames, and were strolling about in the cool salty air near the timber scaffold down which the mineral water continuously flows. I was wearing my new black straw hat with the green ribbon which I had bought at Tauber's in Würzburg, where Leo was now reading classics. It was a beautiful day, and as we were walking along the paths a huge shadow suddenly fell upon us. We looked up at the sky, at the same time as all the other summer guests out walking by the frames, and there was a gigantic zeppelin gliding soundlessly through the blue air, apparently only just clearing the tops of the trees. Everyone was amazed, and a young man standing nearby took that as an excuse to talk to us – taking his courage in both hands, as he later admitted to me. His name, he told us right away, was Fritz Waldhof, and he played the French horn in the spa orchestra, which consisted chiefly of members of the Wiener Konzertverein who took jobs at Kissingen during the summer break every year. Fritz, for whom I had an instant liking, saw us home that afternoon, and the following week we went on our first outing together. Again it was a glorious summer day. I walked ahead with Fritz, and Laura, who had distinct doubts about him, followed with a Hamburg cellist named Hansen. Needless to say, I no longer remember what we talked about. But I do remember that the fields on either side of the path were full of flowers and that I was happy, and oddly enough I also recall that, not far out of town, just where the sign to Bodenlaube is, we overtook two very refined Russian gentlemen, one of whom (who looked particularly majestic) was speaking seriously to a boy of about ten who had been chasing butterflies and had lagged so far behind that they had had to wait for him. This warning can't have had much effect, though, because whenever we happened to look back we saw the boy running about the meadows with upraised net, exactly as before. Hansen later claimed that he had recognized the elder of the two distinguished Russian gentlemen as Muromzev, the president of the first Russian parliament, who was then staying in Kissingen.

I spent the years which followed that summer in the usual way, doing my household duties, handling the accounts and correspondence in the stables and provisioning business, and waiting for the Viennese horn player to return to

Kissingen, which he did regularly, together with the swallows. Over the nine months of separation each year we always grew apart somewhat, despite the many letters we wrote, and so it took Fritz, who like myself was essentially an undemonstrative person, a long time before he proposed to me. It was just before the end of the 1913 season, on a September afternoon that trembled with limpid loveliness. We were sitting by the salt-frames and I was eating bilberries with sour cream from a china bowl, when suddenly Fritz, in the middle of a carefully worked out reminiscence of our first outing to Bodenlaube, broke off and asked me, without further ado, if I should like to marry him. I did not know what to reply, but I nodded, and, though everything else around me blurred, I saw that long-forgotten Russian boy as clearly as anything, leaping about the meadows with his butterfly net; I saw him as a messenger of joy, returning from that distant summer day to open his specimen box and release the most beautiful red admirals, peacock butterflies, brimstones and tortoiseshells to signal my final liberation. Father, however, was reluctant to agree to a speedy engagement. He was not only troubled by the rather uncertain prospects of a French horn player, but also claimed that the proposed attachment was bound to cut me off from the Jewish faith. In the end it was not so much my own petitioning as the unceasing diplomatic efforts of Mother, who was not so concerned about upholding our traditional life, that won the day; and the following May, on my and Leo's twenty-fifth birthday, we celebrated our engagement at a small family gathering. A few months later, however, my dearest Fritz, who had been called up into the Austrian Musicians' Corps and transferred to Lemberg, suffered a stroke in the midst of playing the *Freischütz* overture for the garrison's officers, and fell lifeless from his chair. His death was described to me a few days later in a telegram of condolence from Vienna, and for weeks the words and letters danced before my eyes in all sorts of new combinations. I really cannot say how I went on living, or how I got over the terrible pain of parting that tormented me day and night after Fritz's death, or indeed whether I have ever got over it. At all events, throughout the war I worked as a nurse with Dr Kosilowski. All the spa buildings and sanatoria in Kissingen were full of the wounded and the convalescent. Whenever a new arrival reminded me of Fritz, in appearance or manner, I would be overwhelmed afresh by my tragedy, and that may be why I looked after those young men so well, some of whom were very seriously injured – as if by doing so I might still save the life of my horn player. In May 1917 a contingent of badly wounded artillerymen was brought in, among them a lieutenant whose eyes were bandaged up. His name was Friedrich Frohmann, and I would sit at his bedside long after my duties were over, expecting some kind of a miracle. It was several months before he could open his seared eyes again. As I had guessed, they were Fritz's greyish-green eyes; but extinguished and blind. At Friedrich's request we soon began to play chess, describing the moves we had made or wanted to make in words – bishop to d6, rook to f4, and so on. By an extraordinary feat of memory, Friedrich was soon able to retain the most complex games; and if his memory did fail him, he resorted to his sense of touch. Whenever his fingers moved across the pieces, with a delicate care that I found devastating, I was always reminded of the fingers of my horn player moving upon the keys of his instrument. As the year neared its end, Friedrich came down with some unidentifiable infection and died of it within a fortnight. It was almost the death of me, too, as they later told me. I lost all my beautiful hair and over a quarter of my body weight, and for a long time I lay in a profound, ebbing and flowing delirium in which all I saw was Fritz and Friedrich, and myself, alone, separate from the two of them. To what it was that I owed thanks for my utterly unexpected recovery late that winter, or whether "thanks" is at all the right word, I know as little as I know how one gets through this life. Before the war's end I was awarded the Ludwig Cross in recognition of what they called my self-sacrificing devotion to duty. And then one day the war really was over. The troops came home. The revolution broke out in Munich. The Freikorps soldiers gathered their forces in Bamberg. Eisner was assassinated by Anton Arco Valley. Munich was re-taken and martial law was imposed. Landauer was killed, young Egelhofer and Leviné were shot, and Toller was locked up in a fortress. When everything was finally back to normal and it was business more or less as usual, my parents decided that now was the time to find me a husband, to take my mind off things. Before long, a Jewish marriage broker from Würzburg by the name of Brisacher introduced my present husband, Fritz Ferber, to our home. He came from a Munich family of livestock traders, but was himself just in the process of setting himself up in middle-class life as a dealer in fine art. Initially I consented to become engaged to Fritz Ferber solely because of his name, though later I did come to esteem and love him more with every day. Like the horn player before him, Fritz Ferber liked to take long walks out of town, and, again like him, he was by nature shy but essentially cheerful. In the summer of 1921, soon after our marriage, we went to the

Allgäu, and Fritz took me up the Ifen, the Himmelsschrofen and the Hohes Licht. We looked down into the valleys – the Ostrachtal, the Illertal and the Walsertal – where the scattered villages were so peaceful it was as if nothing evil had ever happened anywhere on earth. Once, from the summit of the Kanzelwand, we watched a bad storm far below us, and when it had passed the green meadows gleamed in the sunshine and the forests steamed like an immense laundry. From that moment I knew for certain that I was now Fritz Ferber's and that I would be glad to work at his side in the newly established Munich picture gallery. When we returned from the Allgäu we moved into the house in Sternwartstrasse where we still live. It was a radiant autumn, and a hard winter to follow. True, it did not snow much, but for weeks on end the Englischer Garten was a miracle of hoar frost such as I had never seen, and on the Theresienwiese they opened up an ice-rink for the first time since the outbreak of war, where Fritz and I would skate in wonderful, sweeping curves, he in his green jacket and I in my fur-trimmed coat. When I think

back to those days, I see shades of blue everywhere – a single empty space, stretching out into the twilight of late afternoon, crisscrossed by the tracks of ice-skaters long vanished.

The memoirs of Luisa Lanzberg have been very much on my mind since Ferber handed them over to me, so much so that in late June 1991 I felt I should make the journey to Kissingen and Steinach. I travelled via Amsterdam, Cologne and Frankfurt, and had to change a number of times, and sit out lengthy waits in the Aschaffenburg and Gemünden station buffets, before I reached my destination. With every change the trains were slower and shorter, till at last, on the stretch from Gemünden to Kissingen, I found myself in a train (if that is the right word) that consisted only of an engine and a single carriage – something I had not thought possible. Directly across from me, even though there were plenty of seats free, a fat, square-headed man of perhaps fifty had plumped himself down. His face was flushed and blotched with red, and his eyes were very close-set and slightly squint. Puffing noisily, he dug his unshapely tongue, still caked with bits of food, around his half-open mouth. There he sat, legs apart, his stomach and gut stuffed horribly into summer shorts. I could not say whether the physical and mental deformity of my fellow-passenger was the result of long psychiatric confinement, some innate debility, or simply beer-drinking and eating between meals. To my considerable relief the monster got out at the first stop after Gemünden, leaving me quite alone in the carriage but for an old woman on the other side of the aisle who was eating an apple so big that the full hour it took till we reached Kissingen was barely enough for her to finish it. The train followed the bends of the river, through the grassy valley. Hills and woods passed slowly, the shadows of evening settled upon the countryside, and the old woman went on dividing up the apple, slice by slice, with the penknife she held open in her hand, nibbling the pieces, and spitting out the peel onto a paper napkin in her lap. At Kissingen there was only one single taxi in the deserted street outside the station. In answer to my question, the driver told me that at that hour the spa clientèle were already tucked up in bed. The hotel he drove me to had just been completely renovated in the neo-imperial style which is now inexorably taking hold throughout Germany and which discreetly covers up with light shades of green and gold leaf the lapses of taste committed in the postwar years. The lobby was as deserted as the station forecourt. The woman at reception, who had something of the mother superior about her, sized me up as if she were expecting me to disturb the peace, and when I got into the lift I found myself facing a weird old couple who stared at me with undisguised hostility, if not horror. The woman was holding a small plate in her claw-like hands, with a few slices of *wurst* on it. I naturally assumed that they had a dog in their room, but the next morning, when I saw them take up two tubs of raspberry yoghurt and something from the breakfast bar that they had wrapped in a napkin, I realized that their supplies were intended not for some putative dog but for themselves.

I began my first day in Kissingen with a stroll in the grounds of the spa. The ducks were still asleep on the lawn, the white down of the poplars was drifting in the air, and a few early bathers were wandering along the sandy paths like lost souls. Without exception, these people out taking their painfully slow morning constitutionals were of pensioner age, and I began to fear that I would be condemned to spend the rest of my life amongst the patrons of Kissingen, who were in all likelihood preoccupied first and foremost with the state of their bowels. Later I sat in a café, again surrounded by elderly people, reading the Kissingen newspaper, the *Saale-Zeitung*. The quote of the day, in the so-called Calendar column, was from Johann Wolfgang von Goethe, and read: *Our world is a cracked bell that no longer sounds.* It was the 25th of June. According to the paper, there was a crescent moon and the anniversary of the birth of Ingeborg Bachmann, the Austrian poet, and of the English writer George Orwell. Other dead birthday boys whom the newspaper remembered were the aircraft builder Willy Messerschmidt (1898–1978), the rocket pioneer Hermann Oberath (1894–1990), and the East German author Hans Marchwitza (1890–1965). The death announcements, headed *Totentafel*, included that of retired master butcher Michael Schultheis of Steinach (80). He was extremely popular. He was a staunch member of the Blue Cloud Smokers' Club and the Reservists' Association. He spent most of his leisure time with his loyal alsatian, Prinz. –

Pondering the peculiar sense of history apparent in such notices, I went to the town hall. There, after being referred elsewhere several times and getting an insight into the perpetual peace that pervades the corridors of small-town council chambers, I finally ended up with a panic-stricken bureaucrat in a particularly remote office, who listened with incredulity to what I had to say and then explained where the synagogue had been and where I would find the Jewish cemetery. The earlier temple had been replaced by what was known as the new synagogue, a ponderous turn-of-the-century building in a curiously orientalized, neo-romanesque style, which was vandalized during the Kristallnacht and then completely demolished over the following weeks. In its place in Maxstrasse, directly opposite the back entrance of the town hall, is now the labour exchange. As for the Jewish cemetery, the official, after some rummaging in a key deposit on the wall, handed me two keys with orderly labels, and offered me

the following somewhat idiosyncratic directions: you will find the Israelite cemetery if you proceed southwards in a straight line from the town hall for a thousand paces till you get to the end of Bergmannstrasse. When I reached the gate it turned out that neither of the keys fitted the lock, so I climbed the

wall. What I saw had little to do with cemeteries as one thinks of them; instead, before me lay a wilderness of graves, neglected for years, crumbling and gradually sinking into the ground amidst tall grass and wild flowers under the shade of trees, which trembled in the slight movement of the air. Here

and there a stone placed on the top of a grave witnessed that someone must have visited one of the dead – who could say how long ago. It was not possible to decipher all of the chiselled inscriptions, but the names I could still read – Hamburger, Kissinger, Wertheimer, Friedländer, Arnsberg, Auerbach, Grunwald, Leuthold, Seeligmann, Frank, Hertz, Goldstaub, Baumblatt and Blumenthal – made me think that perhaps there was nothing the Germans begrudged the Jews so much as their beautiful names, so intimately bound up with the country they lived in and with its language. A shock of recognition shot through me at the grave of Maier Stern,

who died on the 18th of May, my own birthday; and I was touched, in a way I knew I could never quite fathom, by the symbol of the writer's quill on the stone of Friederike Halbleib, who departed this life on the 28th of March 1912. I imagined her pen in hand, all by herself, bent with bated breath over her work; and now, as I write these lines, it feels as if *I* had lost her, and as if *I* could not get over the loss despite the many years that have passed since her departure. I stayed in the Jewish cemetery till the afternoon, walking up and down the rows of graves, reading the names of the dead, but it was only when I was about to leave that I discovered a more recent gravestone, not far from the locked gate, on which were the names of Lily and Lazarus Lanzberg, and of Fritz and Luisa Ferber. I assume Ferber's Uncle Leo had had it erected there. The inscription says that Lazarus Lanzberg died in Theresienstadt in 1942, and that Fritz and Luisa were deported, their fate unknown, in November 1941. Only Lily, who took her own life, lies in that grave. I stood before it for some time, not knowing what I should think; but before I left I placed a stone on the grave, according to custom.

Although I was amply occupied, during my several days in Kissingen and in Steinach (which retained not the slightest trace of its former character), with my research and with the writing itself, which, as always, was going laboriously, I felt increasingly that the mental impoverishment and lack of memory that marked the Germans, and the efficiency with which they had cleaned everything up, were beginning to affect my head and my nerves. I therefore decided to leave sooner than I had planned, a decision which was the easier to take since

Motorbootfahrt Bad Kissingen - Saline G.m.b.H.

Rückfahrkarte

1934

Fahrzeiten siehe Fahrpläne. Fahrpreis siehe Tarif.

Fahrkarte aufbewahren u. auf Verlangen vorzeigen.

my enquiries, though they had produced much on the general history of Kissingen's Jewry, had brought very little to light concerning the Lanzberg family. But I must still say something about the trip I took up to the salt-frames in a motor launch that was moored at the edge of the spa grounds. It was about one o'clock on the day before I left, at an hour when the spa visitors were eating their diet-controlled lunches, or indulging in unsupervised gluttony in gloomy restaurants, that I went down to the riverbank and boarded the launch. The woman who piloted the launch had been waiting in vain, till that moment, for even a single passenger. This lady, who generously allowed me to take her picture, was from Turkey, and had already been working for the Kissingen river authority for a number of years. In addition to the captain's cap that sat jauntily on her

head, she was wearing a blue and white jersey dress which was reminiscent (at least from a distance) of a sailor's uniform, by way of a further concession to her office. It soon turned out that the mistress of the launch was not only expert at manoeuvring her craft on the narrow river but also had views on the way of the world that were worth considering. As we headed up the Saale she gave me a few highly impressive samples of her critical philosophy, in her somewhat Turkish but nonetheless very flexible German, all of which culminated in her oft-repeated point that there was no end to stupidity, and nothing as dangerous. And people in Germany, she said, were just as stupid as the Turks, perhaps even stupider. She was visibly pleased to find a sympathetic ear for her views, which she shouted above the pounding of the diesel engine and underlined with an imaginative repertoire of gestures and facial expressions; she rarely had the opportunity to talk to a passenger, she said, let alone one with a bit of sense. The boat ride lasted some twenty minutes. When it was over, we parted with a shake of hands and, I believe, a certain mutual respect. The salt-frames, which I had only seen in an old photograph before, were a short distance upriver, a little way off in the fields. Even at first glance, the timber building was an overwhelming construction, about two hundred metres long and surely twenty metres high, and yet, as I learnt from information displayed in a glass-fronted case, it was merely part of a complex that had once been far more extensive. There was currently no access – notices by the steps explained that the previous year's hurricane had made structural examinations necessary – but, since there was no one around who might have denied me permission, I climbed up to the gallery that ran along the entire complex at a height of about five metres.

From there one could take a close look at the blackthorn twigs that were bunched in layers as high as the roof. Mineral water raised by a cast-iron pumping station was running down them, and collecting in a trough under the frame.

Completely taken aback both by the scale of the complex and by the steady mineral transformation wrought upon the twigs by the ceaseless flow of the water, I walked up and down the gallery for a long time, inhaling the salty air, which the

slightest breath of air loaded with myriad tiny droplets. At length I sat down on a bench in one of the balcony-like landings off the gallery, and all that afternoon immersed myself in the sight and sound of that theatre of water, and in ruminations about the long-term and (I believe) impenetrable process which, as the concentration of salts increases in the water, produces the very strangest of petrified or crystallized forms, imitating the growth patterns of Nature even as it is being dissolved.

During the winter of 1990/91, in the little free time I had (in other words, mostly at the so-called weekend and at night), I was working on the account of Max Ferber given above. It was an arduous task. Often I could not get on for hours or days at a time, and not infrequently I unravelled what I had done, continuously tormented by scruples that were taking tighter hold and steadily paralysing me. These scruples concerned not only the subject of my narrative, which I felt I could not do justice to, no matter what approach I tried, but also the entire questionable business of writing. I had covered hundreds of pages with my scribble, in pencil and ballpoint. By far the greater part had been crossed out, discarded, or obliterated by additions. Even what I ultimately salvaged as a "final" version seemed to me a thing of shreds and patches, utterly botched. So I hesitated to send Ferber my cut-down rendering of his life; and, as I hesitated, I heard from Manchester that Ferber had been taken to Withington Hospital with pulmonary emphysema. Withington Hospital was a one-time Victorian workhouse, where the homeless and unemployed had been subjected to a strict regime. Ferber was in a men's ward with well over twenty beds, where much muttering and groaning went on, and doubtless a good deal of dying. He clearly found it next to impossible to use his voice, and so responded to what I said only at lengthy intervals, in an attempt at speech that sounded like the rustle of dry leaves in the wind. Still, it was plain enough that he felt his condition was something to be ashamed of and had resolved to put it behind him as soon as possible, one way or another. He was ashen, and the weariness kept getting the better of him. I stayed with him for perhaps three quarters of an hour before taking my leave and walking the long way back through the south of the city, along the endless streets – Burton Road, Yew Tree Road, Claremont Road, Upper Lloyd Street, Lloyd Street North – and through the deserted Hulme estates, which had been rebuilt in the early Seventies and had now been left to fall down

again. In Higher Cambridge Street I passed warehouses where the ventilators were still revolving in the broken windows.

I had to cross beneath urban motorways, over canal bridges and wasteland, till at last, in the already fading daylight, the façade of the Midland Hotel appeared before me, looking like some fantastic fortress. In recent years, ever since his income had permitted, Ferber had rented a suite there, and I too had taken a room for this one night. The Midland was built in the late nineteenth century, of chestnut-coloured bricks and chocolate-coloured glazed ceramic tiles which neither soot nor acid rain have been able to touch. The building runs to three basement levels, six floors above ground, and a total of no fewer than six hundred rooms, and was once famous throughout the land for its luxurious plumbing. Taking a shower there was was like standing out in a monsoon. The brass and copper pipes, which were always highly polished, were so capacious that one of the bathtubs (three metres long and one metre wide) could be filled in just twelve seconds. Moreover, the Midland was renowned for its palm courtyard and, as various sources tell, for its hothouse atmosphere, which brought out both the guests and the staff in a sweat and generally conveyed the impression that here, in the heart of this northern city with its perpetual cold wet gusts, one was in fact on some tropical isle of the blessed, reserved for mill owners, where even the clouds in the sky were made of cotton, as it were. Today the Midland is on the brink of ruin. In the glass-roofed lobby, the reception rooms, the stairwells, the lifts and the corridors one rarely encounters either a hotel guest or one of the chambermaids or waiters who prowl about like sleepwalkers. The legendary steam heating, if it works at all, is erratic; fur flakes from out of the taps; the window panes are coated in thick grime marbled by rain; whole tracts of the building are closed off; and it is presumably only a matter of time before the Midland closes its doors and is sold off and transformed into a Holiday Inn.

When I entered my room on the fifth floor I suddenly felt as if I were in a hotel somewhere in Poland. The old-

fashioned interior put me curiously in mind of a faded wine-red velvet lining, the inside of a jewellery box or violin case. I kept my coat on and sat down on one of the plush armchairs in the corner bay window, watching darkness fall outside. The rain that had set in at dusk was pouring down into the gorges of the streets, lashed by the wind, and down below the black taxis and double-decker buses were moving across the shining tarmac, close behind or beside each other, like a herd of elephants. A constant roar rose from below to my place by the window, but there were also moments of complete silence from time to time. In one such interval (though it was utterly impossible) I thought I heard the orchestra tuning their instruments, amidst the usual scraping of chairs and clearing of throats, in the Free Trade Hall next door; and far off, far, far off in the distance, I also heard the little opera singer who used to perform at Liston's Music Hall in the Sixties, singing long extracts from *Parsifal* in German. Liston's Music Hall was in the city centre, not far from Piccadilly Gardens, above a so-called Wine Lodge where the prostitutes would take a rest and where they had Australian sherry on tap, in big barrels. Anyone who felt the urge could get up on the stage at that music hall and, with the swathes of smoke drifting, perform the piece of his choice to a very mixed and often heavily intoxicated audience, accompanied on the Wurlitzer by a lady who invariably wore pink tulle. As a rule the choice fell upon folk ballads and the sentimental hits that were currently in vogue. *The old home town looks the same as I step down from the train*, began the favourite of the winter season of 1966 to 1967. *And there to greet me are my Mama and Papa.* Twice a week, at a late hour when the heaving mass of people and voices verged on the infernal, the heroic tenor known as Siegfried, who cannot have been more than one metre fifty tall, would take the stage. He was in his late forties, wore a herringbone coat that reached almost to the floor and on his head a Homburg tilted back. He would sing *O weh, des Höchsten Schmerzenstag* or *Wie dünkt mich doch die Aue heut so schön* or some other impressive arioso, not hesitating to act out stage directions such as "Parsifal is on the point of fainting" with the required theatricality. And now, sitting in the Midland's turret room above the abyss on the fifth floor, I heard him again for the first time since those days. The sound came from so far away that it was as if he were walking about behind the wing flats of an infinitely deep stage. On those flats, which in truth did not exist, I saw, one by one, pictures from an exhibition that I had seen in Frankfurt the year before. They were colour photographs, tinted with a greenish-blue or reddish-brown, of the Litzmannstadt ghetto that was established in 1940 in the Polish industrial centre of Lodz, once known as *polski*

Manczester. The photographs, which had been discovered in 1987 in a small suitcase, carefully sorted and inscribed, in an antique dealer's shop in Vienna, had been taken as personal souvenirs by a book-keeper and financial expert named Genewein, who came from near Salzburg and who was himself in one of the pictures, counting money at his bureau. The pictures also showed the lord mayor of Litzmannstadt, one Hans Biebow, on his birthday, well scrubbed and with a neat parting, at a table adorned with asparagus ferns and groaning beneath potted plants, bouquets, cakes and cold cuts. There were German men too with their girlfriends and wives, all – without exception – in high spirits. And there were pictures of the ghetto – street cobbles, tram tracks, housefronts, hoardings, demolition sites, fire protection walls, beneath a sky that was grey, watery green, or white and blue – strangely deserted pictures, scarcely one of which showed a living soul, despite the fact that at times there were as many as a hundred and seventy thousand people in Litzmannstadt, in an area of no more than five square kilometres. The photographer had also recorded the exemplary organization within the ghetto: the postal system, the police, the courtroom, the fire brigade, soil disposal, the hairdresser's, the medical services, the laying out of the dead, and the burial ground. More important to him than anything else, apparently, was to show "our industry", the ghetto works that were essential to the wartime economy. In these production sites, most of which were designed for basic manufacture, women were sitting making baskets, child apprentices were busy in the metalwork shop, men were making bullets or working in the nail factory or the rag depot, and everywhere there were faces, countless faces, who looked up from their work (and were permitted to do so) purposely and solely for the fraction of a second that it took to take the photograph. Work is our only course, they said. – Behind the perpendicular frame of a loom sit three young women, perhaps aged twenty. The irregular geometrical patterns of the carpet they are knotting, and even its colours, remind me of the settee in our living room at home. Who the young women are I do not know. The light falls on them from the window in the background, so I cannot make out their eyes clearly, but I sense that all three of them are looking across at me, since I am standing on the very spot where Genewein the accountant stood with his camera. The young woman in the middle is blonde and has the air of a bride about her. The weaver to her left has inclined her head a little to one side, whilst the woman on the right is looking at me with so steady and relentless a gaze that I cannot meet it for long. I wonder what the three women's names were – Roza, Luisa and Lea, or Nona, Decuma and Morta, the daughters of night, with spindle, scissors and thread.

Also available in Vintage

Robert Hughes

THE FATAL SHORE

'An extraordinary, vivid yet authentic account of the birthpangs of a nation. A work of real distinction'
Philip Ziegler

'A unique phantasmagoria of crime and punishment, which combines the shadowy terrors of Goya with the tumescent life of Dickens'
Peter Ackroyd, *The Times*

'Hughes has a story to tell as vivid, large-scale, and appaling as anything by Dickens or Solzhenitsyn, but one that's virtually unknown – until the writing of this splendid book. *The Fatal Shore* is a great achievement'
Susan Sontag

'A triumph of research, passion and fine writing. I found it an extraordinary and compelling book to read, one of fantastic scope and imagination; truly a *tour de force*'
William Shawcross

'An enthralling account of the convict settlement of Australia, thoroughly researched and excellently written, brimming over with rare and pungent characters, and tales of pathos, bravery, and horror'
Peter Matthiessen

'Popular history in the best sense... its attention to human detail and its commanding prose call to mind the best work of Barbara Tuchman;
Washinton Post

'With its mood and stature... *The Fatal Shore* is well on its way to becoming the standard opus on the convict years'
Sydney Sunday Herald

Also available in Vintage

Boris Pasternak

DOCTOR ZHIVAGO

Winner of the Nobel Prize for Literature

'The first work of genius to come out of Russia
since the Revolution'
V.S. Pritchett

'One of the great events in man's literary and moral history'
Edmund Wilson

Doctor Zhivago is the epic novel of Russia in the throes of revolution and one of the greatest love stories ever told. Yury Zhivago, physician and poet, wrestles with the new order and confronts the changes cruel experience has made in him and the anguish of being torn between the love of two women.

'...[belongs] to that small group of novels by which all others are ultimately judged'
Frank Kermode, *Spectator*

'A book that made a most profound impression on me and the memory of which still does... not since Shakespeare has love been so fully, vividly, scrupulously and directly communicated... The novel is a total experience, not parts or aspects: of what other twentieth-century work of the imagination could this be said?'
Isaiah Berlin, *Sunday Times*

Also available in Vintage

W.G. Sebald

VERTIGO

'One of the most original voices to have come from Europe in recent years'
Paul Auster

'Nothing like *Vertigo* is likely to be encountered in the course of one's regular reading. One emerges from it shaken, seduced and deeply impressed'
Anita Brookner, *Spectator*

'Where has one heard in English a voice of such confidence and precision, so direct in its expression of feeling, yet so respectfully devoted to "the real"?'
Susan Sontag, *Times Literary Supplement*

Part fiction, part travelogue, the narrator of this compelling masterpiece pursues his solitary, eccentric course from England to Italy and beyond, succumbing to the vertiginous unreliability of memory itself.

'Possessed of a richness and strangeness that would put most other writers to shame... Sebald's journey into himself and his past is compelling, puzzling, unique'
The Times

'As a reader, you find his prose wrapping itself, wraith-like, round your imagination, casting a baffling and indefinable spell... it works triumphantly well... the fact that W.G. Sebald chooses to tease, dazzle and mystify should not blind us to the fact that he does the one thing that every novelist should do: he entertains, provokes, stimulates and inspires'
Robert McCrum, *Observer*

Also available in Vintage

W.G. Sebald

THE RINGS OF SATURN

'A great, strange and moving work'
James Wood, *Guardian*

'The finest book of long-distance mental travel that I've ever read'
Jonathan Raban, *Times Literary Supplement*

'A desperate intensity of feeling is thrillingly counterpoised by the workings of a wonderfully learned and rigorous mind'
Sunday Times

The Rings of Saturn begins as the record of a journey on foot through coastal East Anglia. From Lowestoft to Southwold to Bungay, Sebald's own story becomes the conductor of evocations of people and cultures past and present: of Chateaubriand, Thomas Browne, Swinburne and Conrad, of fishing fleets, skulls and silkworms. The result is a book unlike any other in contemporary literature, an intricately patterned and endlessly thought-provoking meditation on the transience of all things human.

'Sebald is surely a major European author... he reaches the heights of epiphanic beauty only encountered normally in the likes of Proust'
Independent on Sunday

'Sebald's exquisitely written philosophical tramp around East Anglia has you asking questions about truth, art and history at every turn of his mysterious path. What's never in doubt is the strength of Sebald's vision or the beauty of his prose'
Boyd Tonkin, *Independent*